A Daughter's Lament

A Daughter's Lament

Lee Gander

RESOURCE *Publications* · Eugene, Oregon

A DAUGHTER'S LAMENT

Resource Publications
An Imprint of Wipf and Stock Publishers
199 W. 8th Ave., Suite 3
Eugene, OR 97401

www.wipfandstock.com

PAPERBACK ISBN: 978-1-6667-4598-6
HARDCOVER ISBN: 978-1-6667-4599-3
EBOOK ISBN: 978-1-6667-4600-6

MAY 31, 2022 8:37 AM

This book is dedicated to Mary Vesperman. Her skill and tireless effort in taking a scattered assortment of anecdotes, stories and unvarnished ideas in the first manuscript of this trilogy, *A Mother's Lament*, brought to life its profound and beautiful redemptive message.

Contents

Author's Note: The Soul vii

Prologue: What if . . . ? x

CHAPTER 1
Resolve 1

CHAPTER 2
Piper's World 7

CHAPTER 3
Finding William C. Clark
Part 1: Preparations 11

CHAPTER 4
Finding William C. Clark
Part 2: The Search Begins 21

CHAPTER 5
Finding William C. Clark
Part 3: Alan and Joe's World 30

CHAPTER 6
Finding William C. Clark
Part 4: Into the Jungle 39

CHAPTER 7
Finding William C. Clark
Part 5: Unexpected Disaster 43

CHAPTER 8
Finding William C. Clark
Part 6: Betrayed   49

CHAPTER 9
Finding William C. Clark
Part 7: William C. Clark's World   55

CHAPTER 10
Finding William C. Clark
Part 8: Rescued Too Late   58

CHAPTER 11
Frank Tells Piper a Story   65

CHAPTER 12
The Cure   72

CHAPTER 13
Finally Home   77

CHAPTER 14
Rude Awakening   82

CHAPTER 15
Deja-vu   87

CHAPTER 16
Finding the Real Dr. William C. Clark   92

CHAPTER 17
Confessions   97

CHAPTER 18
Dr. William Christopher Clark Jr.   101

CHAPTER 19
Not a Wasted Dream   106

CHAPTER 20
The Ultimate Cure   110

Biography   121

Author's Note

The Soul

"THE HEART BEATS, THE lungs breathe, the body hungers and thirsts, the flesh seeks pleasure and reels from pain; emotion endlessly fluctuates from the depths of despair and sorrow to the heights of joy and exhilaration. But I, the soul, lost in this chaos of distractions, continue to softly but relentlessly whisper, 'Heart, you will cease to beat; Lungs, your breath will stop; Body, you will turn to dust; Passion, you will fade away, but I, your Soul, will live on and on and on for eternity.'

"Mind, I patiently long to get your attention, before time brings your thinking to an end; yet seldom do you give me a thought! I continue to tug against the ever-present throng of worldly cares and pleasures and ask, 'what will you do about me? Are you even aware that I'm here? Do you realize that I am the eternal part of your being?'

"Long after everything else has been consumed and disappears, I will be. The body spends all its energy on the momentary needs and desires of this temporary life; in vanity it exercises, builds and plans—but what value does it place on me? When will the wasting away give priority to the eternal?

"I pray that my existence will be realized and proper redemptive action taken, before it is too late!"

Some, especially in the scientific world, say there is no soul, no unique difference between life forms except random biological traits. Yet, to even the casual observer, our human existence is strikingly different from all other life forms. They, the scientists, contend there is consciousness, but only in the physical mind. They contend that we are just an accident of the universe, no soul, no spirit, no future beyond what we see. Still, can they clearly explain what makes humans so different from all other living creatures?

What is this intelligence and drive that humans have to strive for higher and higher levels of creativity and advancement? Why do birds not learn to build better and more complex nests from generation to generation; or beavers, after millions of years (so they say), still build their dams in the same way? Why have they not evolved into building dams with concrete forms and pumps? What makes humans so very different, that in the span of a few thousand years, we've advanced from caves and earthen dwellings to skyscrapers, computers and smart phones?

"In the beginning . . ." is a good place to start. The Bible says that people were created in God's image (Genesis 1:26). No other element or part of God's creation was given that distinction. Every essence of God is in each and every one of us, but not in other creatures, because only people were specifically created in God's image. That is why we can not only invent and create out of seemingly nothing—like God does—it also explains why we are the only creation that is aware of eternity. God has instilled in us the knowledge and understanding of the universe and eternity, as well as the ability to know who God is personally. Why? Because He created us to have relationships with Him, to communicate with Him, connect with Him, love Him and be loved by Him, and be forever with Him.

For you formed my inward parts; you wove me in my mother's womb. I will give thanks to You for I am fearfully and wonderfully made; wonderful are Your works, and my soul knows it very well. My frame was not hidden from You when I was made in secret, and skillfully wrought in the depths of the earth; Your eyes have seen my unformed substance; and in your book were written the days that were ordained for me, when yet there were not one of them. How precious also are Your thoughts to me, O God! How vast is the sum of them! (Psalm 139:13–17)

Do you know, really know, how special you are and that God has precious thoughts of you? In fact, He has deep feelings of love towards you.

God created people to have free wills, so they could freely love Him or reject Him. This fact alone is proof of an all-powerful Creator; for if there was no Creator to give us free will and self-awareness, we would be living in the shadows of ignorance, like every other animal. We would never comprehend the simplest aspects of His creation, such as fire or the benefits of fire.

The Soul, or our individual identity, is therefore very special, and in turn makes us all very uniquely special. Therefore, each child conceived has been given this God-breathed image and identity, filled with His Spirit the moment he is conceived and begins his life journey. Once there is a seed, it never loses its identity; whether an acorn, pinecone, tulip bulb or kernel of corn. After all, does a kernel of corn stop being a kernel of corn just because it is buried in the ground and out of sight? Once buried, is it magically transformed into a mere biological mass or worthless cell, or does it remain a kernel of corn, maintaining its specific botanical identity?

So it is with a conceived child. Just because the 'seed' is hidden in the 'ground' (womb), that child is immediately identified as a child.

Therefore, every child conceived already has a birth identity, a 'germinating' human Soul and Spirit uniquely his/her own, and is just as alive and real as you and me.

If we value our own lives, how can we hypocritically say we don't value the life of another? Every pre-born baby is a person wanting to live, love and thrive, just as much as any other person.

Prologue

What if . . . ?

EVERY ADVANTAGE WE HAVE has come from the mind of an entre-preneur, a risk taker, someone with a vision beyond what we know. Dreamers, whether for wealth, fame or the greater good of man-kind, have changed our world.

Almost every home has an air-conditioner, a smart phone, computer, car, dishwasher, range, boiler or furnace. Hundreds of thousands of lives are prolonged and made more comfortable by medical innovations that scientists bring into our lives almost daily. How different our lives would be today if Thomas Edison (inventor of the light bulb, phonograph, recording machine, generators, etc.) had never been born. Or how about Alexander Fleming, who dis-covered the benefits of penicillin (Antibiotics); Henry Ford (who pioneered the concept of an assembly line, making products more affordable); Willis H. Carrier invented the modern-day HVAC sys-tem); Charles Babbage (inventor of the first computer), along with hundreds of others?

Of course, we would be ignorant of these life-changing inven-tions and scientific breakthroughs had these individuals never been born. But that is my point. We would never have benefited from these individuals' contributions, if one or all had not been born. What if, thirty years ago, abortion took the life of the very person that would have ultimately found the cure for cancers, and every-one you know and love who has cancer or was lost to cancer, would not be suffering or dying from its effects today? We are completely ignorant of the potential realities of how wonderfully improved our lives might have been, had certain children not been aborted in years past.

No, we will never know the full extent of how those born before us influenced our lives for the better, nor will we ever know the great inventions that didn't occur or the love and friendships never offered us by those taken from us before their time.

The movie classic, It's a Wonderful Life illustrates this possibility; for what if George Bailey had truly never been born? How many lives would have suffered or died in that reality? And how much more rich and wonderful our lives might be today, if past lives had been allowed to flourish and live out their potential?

What if . . . ?

CHAPTER 1

Resolve

"I KNOW IT SOUNDS crazy, but I've made up my mind!" Grace insisted.

"So, on a whim, on the flimsiest of evidence, you're going to travel half-way around the world to meet someone we don't even know; to develop a cure for a nameless disease that some of the world's greatest doctors can't even identify, let alone find a cure for themselves?"

"Well, you may think it's a whim, but I know it's the right thing to do. I feel it deep in my soul; I just know it! There's at least some hope if I go, but if I don't—well, you know perfectly well; if I don't go, she . . . she will die!"

"Hope?" Frank responded in mild frustration. "I don't see any hope in what you're planning. There is only danger and misery, and maybe even your own life! Then I'll lose both of you instead of just one!"

"So, you think it's inevitable then? You've given up all hope?"

"Well," Frank hesitated, "I have accepted what I believe to be the inevitable, because I see nothing more we can do. We've checked out every relevant book in three libraries, practically killed a forest making notes and printing out reams of research, traveled thousands of miles with every little clue, emptied our bank accounts, lost our jobs and wore off half the keys on our computers, researching the smallest of leads, while at the same time, consulting the greatest minds we know in this field! What's left?"

"A miracle and a prayer," Grace answered softly, accompanied by an understanding smile. "As long as she is alive and there's a God in heaven, there's hope, as well as this expedition to find Dr. Clark."

"A man we've never met, who doesn't know us from Adam," Frank retorted. The fear and frustration in his voice was clearly not directed at Grace but came from somewhere deeper in his soul. "We've been working day and night, sacrificing and praying for a miracle or a healing for two years, and for what? Sometimes I wonder if there even is a God!"

"Now, Frank, you don't really mean that. I know you're scared; so am I, and as far as Dr. Clark goes, we know a lot more about him than you think. At the very least, his success in discovering and curing rare diseases."

"I know, Grace. It's just that I love you and Piper so much; the thought of losing you both, well . . ."

"Well?" Grace interrupted respectfully, "With God all things are possible. Trust God, Frank, and don't lose hope; just keep praying for that illusive miracle. Maybe it's time to rest, not from working hard, but from our own understanding of things. There is still so much we don't understand, but the answer is out there; I just know it! Perhaps it will be tomorrow through a phone call, or maybe in the jungles of Africa!"

"Well . . ." Frank hesitated, unconvinced.

"You'll see, we will find that cure yet," Grace said confidently. "And as long as there's a thread of hope, we must keep fighting and have faith."

"Faith?" Frank responded skeptically. "I think this little jungle excursion you've cooked up is madness, and in my humble opinion, doesn't have a prayer!"

"So you don't believe in the power of prayer?" Grace jabbed at Frank whimsically.

"Yes, of course I do. Well, you know what I mean. It's just such a dangerous undertaking, with no guarantee of success." Frank paused and then continued reflectively. "Grace, have you . . . have we . . . truly counted the cost?"

"In my heart I have," Grace answered thoughtfully. "I'm just as afraid of going as you—maybe more; I'm terrified! A hundred miles deep into the African jungle, teeming with mysterious wild animals . . ."

"Not to mention the superstitious tribes in the area with all their head shrinking and cannibalism!" Frank interrupted, shivering.

"I, I am scared, "Grace winced at the thought. "It won't be easy."

"Easy?" Frank reacted incredulously. "We will be lucky if you survive!"

"Let's stop, Frank, for Piper's sake, or I'll lose my nerve. I am committed to going whatever the cost, and that's it! And—well, we won't be trusting in luck, we'll be trusting in God; and as long as our precious Piper keeps fighting, we need to be right there fighting with her."

"Yes, of course," Frank repented sheepishly, knowing better, and knowing he was sounding a little ridiculous at the moment. "I just hope that, well, when you run into a man-eating tiger, a twenty-foot python, or a tribe of head-shrinking cannibals, God will be there to protect you, 'cause I sure won't be! I will feel as helpless here, as a . . ."

"Now, Frank, please be reasonable and don't worry," Grace interrupted with a mischievous smile, trying to lighten the mood. "Anyway, you don't have to worry about 'man-eating' tigers; only 'woman-eating' tigers, and to my knowledge, no one has ever seen one of them, not even in the scariest, darkest jungles of Africa."

Frank at first chuckled at his wife's attempt at humor, and then turned pale as he visualized the all-too-real menace behind the joke. "You joke now, but I am being reasonable! You're putting your life at risk on a seemingly hopeless venture. How can I wholeheartedly support that?"

"You know we have more to go on than just blind hope, Frank," Grace responded positively. "What about all the research that led to finding Dr. Clark, a doctor that has already succeeded in discovering several cures for rare diseases, some with the same type of cellular corruption as Piper's, and is now a hundred miles deep in the jungle working on another?"

"Yes, maybe cures of a similar type," Frank pressed skeptically, "but we still only have a theory, a vague direction; and who's to say he'll even take the time to work on what we need? After all, he's in the middle of his own research and communicated that he was reluctant to work with us, even if you went to him!"

"I will just have to convince him when I get there, that's all. At least we have a direction to pursue that we didn't have even a few weeks ago, and someone whose work parallels ours! In that we have hope; maybe even the answer to our prayers, and the miracle we've been praying for."

"You are truly a brave little genius," Frank said, admiringly. "If anyone can pull it off, I guess with God's help, you can. But still . . ."

"But still, Frank dear," Grace interfered, "how can we get Dr. Clark's help and expertise without getting to him? You know our latest discoveries are sound; we're getting so close, and with Dr. Clark's help, I know we can do it!"

"But . . ." Frank protested, as Grace persisted at holding the high ground.

"Yes, I know he's isolated deep in the jungle, only communicating with his office by mail or through native curriers, and he doesn't even have a S. A.T. phone . . ."

". . . And, he is very reluctant to meet with you, and only on his terms; and only at his compound in Africa."

". . . And, he won't be back in the States for at least a year! That's why I must go now! Piper doesn't have a year; she doesn't even have . . . have . . . months!" Breaking down in a paroxysm of tears with this terrifying thought, Grace looked up at Frank in despair.

"I know," Frank, said sympathetically, affectionately drawing Grace into his comforting arms. "I can see there's no other way, and I can't blame you for wanting to take any risk for our precious baby. My mind knows it's the right think to do, and Piper's only hope, but my heart, Grace, oh, my heart is so torn . . ."

"I know dear, but I feel this is Piper's one last chance."

"I agree, but if I were to lose you both, I . . ."

"Shhh . . ." Grace interrupted sweetly, putting a finger to his lips and placing a tender kiss on his cheek. "If anything happens to me, you and Piper will cherish your last days together, knowing we did all we could to save her. No one can know for sure what is beyond tomorrow," Grace said with a sigh. "Besides, you know both Dad and Alan are going with me; Dad, so creative and logical, and Alan, an avid outdoorsman."

"My sweet Grace, I just want to make sure we've weighed the cost, and know beyond a shadow of a doubt that this is the right thing to do, and that the risk is worth it."

"Worth it?" Grace questioned, getting up and taking Frank by the hand, leading him quietly into Piper's bedroom.

There, surrounded by a plethora of machines, monitors, computers, tubes and wires pulsating rhythmically around her, was an angelic five-year-old girl, sleeping peacefully under a clear plastic oxygen tent, on a comfortable, custom motorized hospital bed.

"She is worth it," Grace whispered quietly, as hot, loving tears trickled down her cheeks.

Frank drew her close again. "Are you prepared to miss the last days of her life if your effort fails?" Frank whispered.

"That has been the hardest and most terrifying thought of all. But if I find him . . . oh, Frank, if I find him and we discover a cure . . ."

"Don't . . . g . . . go." A soft voice strained to speak just then from under the plastic bubble, interrupting Grace.

"Piper dear, did we wake you?" Grace responded apologetically to the trembling voice, as she carefully removed the plastic cover that surrounded her.

"D . . . don't . . . go . . ."

"Do you want us to stay with you for a while?" Frank asked. "Are you lonely?

"Too . . . d . . . dangerous . . ."

"Oh, Piper . . ." Grace sighed, realizing Piper's concern.

"Mama has to go; for your sake," Frank interposed, showing a unified resolve and explaining simply that it was the only remaining course of action.

"Everything will be alright," Grace added reassuringly.

"Miss . . . you . . ." Piper spoke in a whisper, with no little effort, and no few tears in her eyes. She knew what her mother's leaving meant, what she was trying to accomplish by leaving, and the perilous dangers she would face. She also wanted to communicate her strong desire for her mother to stay, even at the expense of her own life, but she had already depleted what little strength she had, silencing her plea.

"I know, Piper dear, I'll miss you too, so very much, but Papa and Grandmamma Gloria will be here with you, and I'll be back soon, hopefully with something to make you feel better and make you well."

Grace's words of comfort and assurance however, were not heard, as Piper drowsily drifted off to sleep again as a result of her mental and physical exertions. Grace lovingly patted dry her daughter's face and tired eyes, and then carefully replaced the clear plastic covering back over her.

"If I could only go with you," Frank implored, as they quietly returned to the living room. "It wouldn't be so . . . so nerve-racking!"

"I know, but we've gone over this before," a resigned Grace answered. "If I were to go, you would be needed here with Piper until I get back. You're somewhat of a genius yourself, you know," Grace quipped playfully, "but, not as qualified as I am to meet with Dr. Clark—no offense." Frank was not offended, as his eyes revealed the love and pride he felt deep in his heart for his lovely, intelligent wife. "Not only that," Grace continued, "there's no one else more qualified, experienced, or that I trust more, to keep our baby alive until I get back."

Frank reflected silently, surrendering his mind to the heart of Grace's passion and resolve.

"We can't both leave her alone at this crucial time, Frank. She needs one of us here; she needs you and my love through you, to sustain and comfort her," Grace concluded.

"You're right of course, but oh, how dreadfully we will miss you."

"I'll miss both of you too, Frank, so very, very much."

CHAPTER 2

Piper's World

PIPER, THE DAUGHTER OF Frank and Grace Connors, was a happy, healthy baby, until just after her third birthday. Grace first noticed some cognitive and behavioral abnormalities, but with Frank's optimistic encouragement, brushed it off as a natural course of child development. However, it wasn't long before it was clear this wasn't the case, and that there was something definitely wrong.

Frank and Grace spent the next two years desperately trying to find the cause of this continued regression of motor function and speech development. Specialist after specialist was consulted with no clear result, other than a consensus that Piper's condition was rare and a mystery. There were many speculations as to what it might be, and though her illness mimicked several known diseases, her unique symptoms remained obscure and continued to frustrate the specialists, and the Connors.

Frank and Grace tried various treatments, along with some of their own modifications. While these methods were substantially able to slow the degenerative process; still, by Piper's fifth birthday she had lost most of her muscular strength and was limited entirely to bed rest inside an oxygen tent. As devastating as this affliction was however, to her parents' great relief, it was evident early on that Piper's condition only affected her physically; mentally she was as alert and intelligent as any other child her age.

Piper's care was the best it could be, with around-the-clock personal attention from the highest recommended professional nursing services, and Grace's mother, Gloria, when a nurse was not available. Initially (and providentially) each of the Connors had prosperous careers in the medical sciences and biomedical fields, aiding them greatly in both the research and financial care of their daughter; though their finances of late had been greatly strained.

For her part, Grace was not just considered a genius; evidenced by graduating high school at the age of sixteen, and from college still in her teens, but far more. She had extensive advanced graduate training, and had almost more letters behind her name than the alphabet. She met Frank in college and soon after married. Though not considered a genius, Frank was bright, creative and very intelligent. Both Frank and Grace were very thankful that their careers were in fields of study best suited to help their daughter fight, and hopefully someday achieve victory over this illusive and still undiagnosed rare disease.

"Frank, look!" Grace cried out one evening while following up on another routine lead from earlier in the day, "You've got to see this!"

Frank closed the book he was reading and hurried over to Grace's side. He knew her find must be a significant breakthrough, as these outbursts of excitement were so rare of late.

Looking more like a research laboratory than a comfortable living space, their living room was set up to expedite their efforts and their colleagues' efforts, to investigate that illusive cure.

It was after a disappointing year of frustration and failure on the part of the experts that Frank and Grace decided to enlist some of their own acquaintances, and take matters into their own hands.

"Look at this scientist's study on isotopes and botanical-based atomic cellular bonding agents, and how they isolate and attack the protein of its organic host!" Grace exclaimed, pointing at an article by Dr. William C. Clark.

"And, it says here," Frank added with equal enthusiasm, as he scanned down the page, "that his method of suppressing this micro-particle strain of the type B influenza virus, increases the quality, volume and density of bone marrow production! That's exactly what Piper needs!

"Frank, this could be it!" Grace said excitedly, after a long review of Dr. Clark's findings in this significant paper, which closely mimicked the area of their own studies. "This doctor's research is as close as we've ever come to finding someone whose work parallels our own!"

"Piper!" Frank yelled, grabbing Grace's hand and rushing her into Piper's room.

"Your mother is a genius!" Frank said breathlessly, while pulling back the oxygen tent, so they could see their beautiful daughter unobstructed. "Mama might have found the answer to making you well, or at least someone who might be able to help us make you well!"

"But Frank, we don't even know who this Dr. Clark is, or whether he is willing to help us or not."

"We'll call the Northern Light Mayo Hospital in the morning for those answers," Frank said, lifting their precious daughter from her bed. "Tonight, we celebrate—and hope!"

Within moments Piper was in her parents' arms, while they planted loving kisses on each of her cheeks. Piper giggled and smiled, joining her parents' enthusiastic celebration over the good news.

"G . . . good news! Sharing her parents' excitement, she beamed and then asked, "Who . . . is Doctor . . . ?"

"The article Mama found was written by a Doctor William C. Clark," Frank answered, saving Piper from the strain of finishing her question. She looked admiringly at her mother.

"Do you . . . kn . . . know . . . him?" Piper asked.

"Not yet, but we will," Grace answered confidently, as they both gently caressed their suffering little child. "He may be the very one, Piper! He may be the one to help us finally solve this dreadful mystery, once and for all!"

"Answer . . . to our p . . . pray . . . ers?

"I hope so, sweetheart," Frank answered, giving Piper another loving kiss on her forehead.

"You know we'll do our best, Piper, dear," Grace added, as they gently lowered Piper back into her bed.

"You . . . always do . . ." Piper said, as a stray tear welled up and trailed down her temple, disappearing into her dark soft curls.

"Love you . . . mommy . . . daddy."

Even this short time of excitement strained Piper's limited energy, so after a brief good night and prayers, the clear plastic canopy was again placed over Piper.

That night there was a rare, fresh ray of hope in the Connors' house by the name of William C. Clark, and for the moment at least, it had broken through the dark shadows of doubt and despair.

"Hope sure is powerful," Grace whispered softly to Frank, as they drifted off into a deeper and more restful sleep than they had known in weeks.

CHAPTER 3

Finding William C. Clark

Part 1: Preparations

"FRANK, HAVE YOU HEARD from Alan? He was supposed to be here an hour ago!" Grace called from the next room.

"Not a word."

"What about Dad?"

"Not a word."

"What about Mom?"

"Not a word."

"What are you doing?"

"What you told me to do."

"What is that?"

"Everything . . ."

"Oh, Frank! This isn't a time for joking around; we have a lot to do!"

"I know, that's what you told me; that's why I'm doing everything," Frank said enduringly as he emerged from the spare room. "Try to relax; they'll be here soon."

Just then the front door swung open wide with a bang, and a painfully ear-bending duet of *O Sole Mio* met their ears. With great fanfare and amid a commotion of song and laughter, Alan, a close family friend, and Grace's father Jim entered triumphantly, looking

11

as though they had just stepped off the jungle set of Indiana Jones, and followed reluctantly by an embarrassed Gloria.

"What is all that?" Grace asked incredulously, as Alan and Jim, adorned in khaki camouflage, fedoras and a myriad of whips, haversacks and pistols, banged their way through the front door as they entered.

"What do you mean my fair maiden?" Grace's father responded, in a mocked voice of astonished offense. "Isn't this the attire that all safari-bound explorers are wearing these days?"

"Dad, you can't be serious! You are so embarrassing sometimes!" Grace exclaimed, as she turned and stormed away toward the bedroom. "Frank, will you talk some sense into your father-in-law and his *explorer* buddy? I have *important* work to do!" And then she added, "This isn't a game, you know!" She slammed the door behind her so hard that it flew back open.

Grace knew she would greatly regret this outburst of emotion one day, but exhausted and stressed over the preparations and uncertainty of what was to come, her self-control had been strained to the limit.

"I told you she wouldn't be impressed with your crazy antics," Gloria muttered, as she entered behind the befuddled, flamboyant duo, following Grace quickly into the bedroom.

"I think you've mixed up your metaphors a little too, gentlemen." Frank added, with a mock snicker. "Shouldn't you be wearing sombreros, or maybe even a Cappella roman, with a song like that?" Another incredulous, frustrated sigh came from the bedroom, as Grace yelled out, "More like a couple of drunk 'Leaning Towers of Pisa', if you ask me!"

Although greatly irritated by her dad and his best friend's frivolity and adolescent behavior, Grace nevertheless saw the humor in it all, which eventually brought a reluctant smile to her face and an affectionate appreciation for their willingness to volunteer for what would most likely be a very dangerous and uncomfortable adventure.

When together, Jim and Alan's behavior was by now notorious and predictable, and it held no secret or surprise for Grace. She had known Alan since she could remember, and knew that her dad and

Alan had become the greatest of friends following the tragic death of her little sister, Jeni.

"How are you holding up, Grace dear?" Gloria asked, as she sat next to her daughter on the bed, slipping a comforting arm around her.

"Oh, Mama . . ." Grace blurted out, sobbing uncontrollably, while turning and throwing herself, shaking in grief, upon her mother's neck. "I'm trying to be strong."

"I know, dear," her mother said soothingly, comforting her distraught and overwhelmed daughter.

"Why do these things happen?" Grace lamented, "What have I done to deserve all this?"

At that instant Gloria thought if anyone deserved anything *bad* to happen to them, it was her, not her daughter, for what she had done to Grace's little sister those many years ago. *Could this be the consequence of my own sin being thrust upon my daughter and granddaughter?* She thought for a fleeting second, but knew better; for she had found the true and lasting forgiveness in the everlasting and powerful arms of Jesus Christ. So, she quickly brushed the thought away, knowing it was a cheap shot from Satan to discourage her at that moment from being an encouragement for her daughter.

"Now, now, everything will be alright; you'll see," Gloria assured her daughter. "God doesn't work that way. If He did, I wouldn't deserve you, or Piper, or anything good in my life; you know that."

"Oh! I'm sorry, Mama!" Grace pulled back with a start. "I didn't mean to bring up . . ."

"No Grace, darling," Gloria interrupted in order to relieve any Freudian-slip offense Grace might have thought she made. "It is impossible to be reminded of what I already think about every day of my life," Gloria reflected, and then to dispel the heavy cloud of gloom that had settled over them, continued, "I still get a kick out of it when you and Frank call her your 'little' sister; she would be almost two years older than you if she were still here with us . . ."

"I can't imagine what you've gone through, Mom," Grace interrupted.

"No, and I know you never will; at least in the same way anyway. Still, God graciously gave me a second chance with you. In a way it's like I've lived Jeni's life all over again through you; and that makes our lives together doubly special."

"Thanks, Mom . . ."

"Oh, hush now, or you'll have us both blubbering like little school children," Gloria said with a reflective sigh. "I've always wondered what it would have been like to have both of you here though. Jeni would have been such a help to you, especially now. You are such a loving and sacrificial mother."

"Well, didn't I learn how to be a mom from you?" Grace volunteered appreciatively. "Besides, you're here, Mama, and you always have been here for me; for all of us. You're amazing, and there couldn't be a more wonderful mom in the entire world . . ."

"Are you two going to blubber in each other's arms all afternoon with so much work yet to be done?" Jim interrupted with a jest, regretting that he had stumbled unexpectedly into such an intimate elevated state of emotion.

"We'll be right there," Gloria and Grace answered simultaneously; wiping away their tears, while an embarrassed Jim removed himself from the doorway as quickly as he had appeared.

"I never met Jeni," Gloria said, getting up to leave in response to Jim's clumsy summons, but still holding Grace's hand. "It would have been so much harder to let her go if I had."

Standing there and looking into her daughter's eyes, Gloria realized she couldn't truly empathize with the fear and apprehension her daughter must have been feeling at that very moment. It was a fact; Gloria had lost her baby, Jeni; and regrettably, by her own choice. But she had never held Jeni, played with her, comforted her, or had a chance to bond with her, as Grace had had with Piper. *How much harder and traumatic it would be,* she thought, *to lose a child so close to one's heart; a child you've held and loved for so many years?*

Unknown to Gloria in that same moment, Grace was thinking how grateful she was to have had a few years with Piper, even if the worst should come; while her mom never even had five minutes to hold and love her precious little Jeni. Neither would ever speak of their mutual laments and empathy toward each other, but hid them lovingly and forever in their hearts.

"What's the latest news, Frank?" Alan asked, as the hilarity of their audacious entrance subsided.

"Can I get you 'king of the jungle' gentlemen anything from the kitchen, before you start solving the world's problems?" Gloria asked, as she emerged from the bedroom, not knowing whether to scold them or laugh hysterically over their little prank.

"Coffee, sure thanks," they answered together.

"Some good and some bad," Frank answered, returning to Alan's question, and putting an emphasis on the *bad*. "According to Joe, our contact in Bondoukou, the authorities are reporting a resurgence of the decades-long civil war in the north with outbreaks of minor skirmishes near the Comoe National Park. Foreigners are being warned not to go out at night and to have an escort with them, even during the daytime."

"Not exactly in the direction we're traveling, but a little too close for comfort," Grace's father pointed out.

"But that isn't the worst of it," Frank continued solemnly.

"There's more?" Alan reacted, astonished. "As if that wasn't enough?"

"According to Joe, there has also been a resurgence of cannibalism and ritual sacrificing in the southern Zorzor region. Now in truth, those areas are hundreds of miles from where we will be, but it's still quite unnerving."

"That explains Grace's reaction to our grandiose entrance," Jim reflected. "I didn't realize . . . I'd better go see how she's doing."

"Well, that's a lot of bad news," Gloria commented to Frank, overhearing their conversation as she returned from the kitchen.

"Yes, I don't see how there's any room left for any good news, with all that bad news cluttering up the place," Alan mused half-heartedly.

"Well, in spite of how bad it sounds, Joe assured me, at least for now, the situation there is stabilizing, and is not serious enough to delay or cancel the expedition," Frank finished with a sigh of relief.

"Not the best news for sure, but it could have been worse," Alan agreed.

"Well, it is what it is," Frank added, "and I'm sure Grace is relieved that it won't push back our start date. Piper is counting on us and this crazy adventure to be successful."

"She is quite a fighter," Alan said admiringly of his little friend in the other room, "but I fear this coming quest to find Dr. Clark is her last hope."

"So, what's the latest on Dr. Clark, anyway?" Jim inquired, returning from checking on Grace.

"Well again, according to his last telegram, the good news is that he's still reluctantly willing to meet with Grace, but of course, he makes no guarantee on the outcome or the amount of time he can spare, due to the time restraints of his own work."

"I'm sorry, Alan, for my reaction earlier," Grace started to say, as she emerged from the bedroom, a few minutes after her father, putting the last stubborn strand of hair back in its place. "I wasn't myself, and, and . . ." Then, with an uncontrollable snort upon seeing again the two arrayed in their over-the-top camouflage kakis, she burst out laughing, her eyes dancing from one to the other. "Really, Dad, Alan?" was all she could manage before another torrent of laughter overcame her.

Grace was normally not prone to having such extreme episodes of uncontrolled emotions, but the mental strain over Piper's care, financial issues, exhaustive research, preparations for this excursion into the unknown, and the disquieting news from the Ivory Coast, had worn her nerves thin.

"No, we're sorry, Gracie; we didn't know about the troubling news from the Ivory Coast until just now," Alan said apologetically.

"Yes, dear, under the circumstances, our foolhardy entrance was in bad taste," Jim agreed.

"No, it's me. I should know better. It's just my nerves," Grace admitted, a little embarrassed after finally conquering her emotions.

"Was Joe able to make all the arrangements on his end?" Grace asked Frank, as the seriousness of the news again became front and center.

"According to his last email, he says it's still a go," Frank began cautiously, "however, he told me the situation is very unstable and could change at any moment."

"Well, I just want to know my little girl will be safe over there," Gloria joined in with a concerned look.

"Oh, don't worry about me, Mom, I'll be fine. How could I not be, with the two *Jones Brothers* here tagging along to protect me from all those wild animals and headhunters?"

After a good laugh over Grace's humorous depiction of her dad and Alan, they all sat down to have a serious discussion, mulling over plans, expressing apprehensions and expectations, and projecting positive as well as potential negative outcomes of their upcoming jungle adventure.

"What is that?" Grace asked the next day, as Alan was loading 'Safari Jane', Alan's old pickup truck.

"Just some stuff that Joe highly recommended we take for the trip."

"No. I mean that specific box you're loading now," Grace said, directing Alan's attention to what was currently in his hands.

"Oh, this?" Alan answered, pointing to a picture on the box. "This is mosquito netting."

"Mosquito netting?"

"Yah, you know, Gracie, for when we're sleeping. It's hard to sleep when there is an army of mosquitoes and other bugs determined to either relieve you of all your blood or haul you away for a late night snack."

"Oh!" Grace shuddered.

"You didn't think we were staying at a 'Best Western' while hiking through the jungle, did you?"

"N . . . no, of course not, but . . ." Grace stammered, as she started to visually contemplate what she was getting into.

"You think the most dangerous thing we will encounter is a lion or a cobra, or some wild beast, but they say the most dangerous thing in the world is a mosquito, especially in the jungle."

Grace, who dreaded bugs more than just about anything, winced and would have turned green if that were truly possible, but the sick look on her face was clear enough.

"Oh, come now, Gracie, it won't be as bad as all that," Alan reassured her matter-of-factly; and then asked, "Is it that urgent that you go with us?"

"Yes," Grace answered with a shiver and a sigh, "but . . ."

"Then, you will be just fine!" Alan cut in confidently, throwing another box of netting into Safari Jane.

"What are all those for?" Grace shrieked, as Alan started loading several boxes of cartridges and a small assortment of pistols and rifles into 'Old Jane'. Grace bent over, steadying herself against Jane's fender.

"For our protection," Alan answered, noting the pale flush of green and spasmodic breathing of the city girl.

"Protection?" Grace asked, turning away from her view of the dreadful things.

Until today, she had only seen guns on television or in a movie; so there was a natural aversion upon seeing the real thing. Grace assumed that their destination would be somewhat dangerous, but when she saw the rifles and ammunition being loaded into Old Jane, the full realization of the true dangers of this little excursion into the jungle became a stark reality.

"Here's some more ammo," Frank offered, walking with Jim up to Alan and handing the cartridge boxes to him.

"Oh good," Alan said, taking the boxes from Frank and putting them with the others.

"What's the matter with Grace?" Jim asked, noticing his daughter slumped over Old Jane's fender.

"She'll be alright in a minute," Alan said, smiling. "I think the reality of what she's signed on for is just starting to sink in."

"Alan, how dangerous do you actually think this trip will be?" Frank asked, starting to share his wife's newfound concern.

"Yes —" Grace interrupted, now somewhat recovered from her shock. "How dangerous will it be?"

"Nothing really to worry about," Alan answered unconvincingly. "We just need to take a few precautions."

Grace wasn't convinced, especially as she caught a wary glace between her father and Alan from the corner of her eye; but she let it go. She knew that no matter the danger, it was for Piper, and for Piper, she would do anything.

Joe from the Comoe National Park staff, had made all the arrangements and was to be their guide to Dr. Clark's compound. Updated reports a few days later regarding the tribal factions and unrest in the area were more positive, and conditions had seemingly improved, to the great relief of the somewhat anxious team.

"Do . . . do you really . . . need . . . to go so . . . so soon . . . ?" Piper asked in painful short breaths, trying to lift her head toward her mother as tears filled her eyes. "I w . . . will . . . miss . . . you."

"It's time," Grace said, touching a loving finger to Piper's lips to encourage her to be still and not over-exert herself. "Just keep praying and thinking about how happy we will both be when I return with the medicine that will make you well."

"I will mam . . . ma . . ." Piper answered weakly; as she relaxed her straining neck, again allowing her head to rest comfortably back on her pillow.

After they all huddled around Piper's bed to have a solemn time of prayer, they left Grace alone to say her special goodbye to Piper.

As she dried the eyes of her precious little girl, Grace noticed for the first time in months that Piper was getting weaker. After a final kiss, Grace turned quickly and walked away as the tears flowed freely. She no longer feared the jungle or the unknown perils, but only the fear of returning too late to save her daughter.

"Are you ready, Grace sweetie?" Her mom asked, as Grace finally emerged from the house, still wiping her tears.

"She's going so, so fast, Mama," Grace lamented, as a new volley of tears flooded her eyes. "What good is it to have all these degrees if they can't help my daughter?"

"Don't worry, honey. Frank and I will take good care of her while you are away," Gloria assured, giving her daughter one last embrace, before she got into Safari Jane. "Just . . . just be safe, and get back as soon as you can." Now it was Gloria's turn to weaken, her eyes moist and swollen.

Safari Jane was finally loaded and ready to go; at least more ready than the apprehensive travelers waiting to climb into her.

Frank said his farewells to Alan and Jim, and then gave his wife one final, passionate kiss goodbye. A tremor of fear came over him as they parted, though for Grace's sake, he portrayed an attitude of calm confidence.

"Goodbye, Alan, Jim," Gloria said, trying to hold back her emotions as she made her rounds from one to the other. "You take good care of my little girl, now."

"We will, with our lives, we will," Alan promised, as Grace, Jim and Alan rolled down the windows of Safari Jane in order to wave their final goodbyes.

A minute later, old Jane had disappeared around the corner at the end of the street. Gloria and Frank walked back to the house in reflective silence, where their special charge was in her special bed waiting for the outcome of her mother's love and courage.

CHAPTER 4

Finding William C. Clark

Part 2: The Search Begins

As EXPECTED, THE FLIGHT to the Bondoukou, Cote D'Ivoire airport, a site located just a few miles from the border of neighboring Ghana, was uneventful. It was after they arrived, however, that things started to go sideways for the wayward, inexperienced explorers. A blast of hot and stifling air greeted them as they stepped from the plane, made even more uncomfortable by a staggering humidity of almost one hundred percent. A series of troubling events began to unfold, and their trust in the Almighty and love for Piper alone, kept them resolved and sane through it all.

First, the authorities confiscated all their firearms and ammunition, and other items deemed to be contraband, even though they had received clear permission through the American Consulate that bringing *defensive* weapons—not *hunting* weapons—was allowed. It was later that they learned this action was taken due to the hostilities and volatile nature of the recent troubling events in the area.

Then, after spending hours pleading with the authorities and filling out paperwork, trying to re-acquire their much-needed defensive weapons, there was the language barrier. Although the tourist trades and officials in Bondoukou spoke relatively good English, the general population outside the metropolitan regions, especially those needed to ferry them from one place to another, spoke very broken English, if any at all.

"How are Frank and little Piper doing, Grace?" Jim asked, as Grace finished getting a quick update on how things were going back home.

"Oh, they're doing just fine for now," Grace answered, with a melancholy voice. "I miss them so much."

"I know, Grace; me too. But we will be home soon, and with a cure."

"Amen to that!" Alan added, as the cabby finished loading up what was left of their gear.

"Where are we to meet this Joe fellow again?" Jim asked Alan, as they left the relatively smooth city roads for the pothole-laden, country dirt paths that the locals insisted were still considered roads.

Hey, look!" Grace interrupted excitedly, pointing out the window.

"Elephants!" Alan cried out.

"A whole herd of them," Grace's father responded in turn, as another herd of Roan antelope farther in the distance ran across a grassy plateau.

"Frank would love this," Grace exclaimed, as all their cell phones went into action to preserve the moment.

"Much to see here," the cabby added with pride, looking back at his passengers with a big, toothless grin. "You see many new things here."

In spite of the unique mountain scenery, animal life, lush open prairies and towering giant leafy trees, there was little comfort on this first leg of their journey. Besides the steady stream of hot air passing through the open windows, the road, if you could call it that, was strewn with numerous boulders, potholes and protruding roots, as the driver veered one way, and then the other, managing to miss only a few of them.

"Yes there is . . . Ouch!" Alan started to answer the cabby, but was abruptly interrupted with a crushing blow to his head against the door frame, as one wheel of the car suddenly dropped into a large pothole, causing the vehicle's occupants to be thrown violently.

"Are you alight, Alan?" Grace inquired, a little concerned as she noticed a trail of blood starting from a gash on his forehead.

"Oh, I'll be fine, once this throbbing goes away," Alan responded, somewhat dazed. "No major damage as far as I can tell."

"Well, at least the authorities didn't confiscate our first-aid kit," Grace said, trying to apply the necessary remedy to Alan's head, with the cab still dipping and swaying erratically.

"So sorry. No good road," the cabby said unsympathetically. "I drive slower now."

True to his word, the cabby did slow down, but his passengers all wondered if by driving slower, the wheels just fell deeper into the ruts and holes, making the already intolerable excursion worse.

Soon however, they arrived at the first leg of their journey, practically worshipping the ground now firmly under their feet. They noticed a stark contrast between the commotion of the city, the roaring motor and rattling of the old rusty cab, to the quiet droning of the jungle noises all about them. From every direction, an echoing chorus of birds called out harmoniously, while a host of chattering monkeys leaped from tree to tree high above them. The thick foliage of underbrush and giant leafy trees fluttered and slapped against each other with a monotonous moaning, as an invisible stiff summer breeze made its way through them. Then, slowly through this already tumultuous din of activity, a plethora of croaking amphibious life and buzzing insects emerged, and joined the ever-active sounds of the dark jungle surrounding them.

"Thank you, thank you," the cabby said with animation through his wide toothless grin, in response to Jim's generous tip. After the cabby unloaded the team's gear, the threesome gathered up their belongings and turned to study more closely the village they had just entered, as the rattling of the cab slowly faded into the distance behind them.

"So this is Tagati of the Zanzan district," Alan murmured, unimpressed with the village, but speechless at the raw beauty of the towering trees and mountain ranges beyond.

"Where are we to meet this Joe person?" Jim questioned, returning to his earlier thoughts, before arriving at the village and before Alan's unwelcome bump on the head.

"According to the itinerary, we are to meet him at the livery stable on the north end of the village," Grace responded to his query.

As they started to look around to get their bearing and ascertain which way was north, thatched-roofed buildings and huts met their gaze, scarcely varying in appearance from one to the other, and with no hint of a main street anywhere.

"S'cuse, please." An old sun-weathered, native gentleman addressed the out-of-place, confused-looking foreigners. "You lost?"

"Well, you might say that," Alan answered with a pleasant smile, turning in the direction of the unfamiliar voice. "We are looking for a man named Joe. We are to meet him at a livery stable north of town."

"Town?" The old man inquired. "What is town?"

"A village," Alan clarified.

"Oh, village. Here is village," he said, pointing at the huts.

"Where is the livery stable?" Alan continued to inquire.

"Livery stable?" The old man again looked puzzled.

"Horses," Alan responded, starting to get a little frustrated with the language barrier; "where people keep horses."

"Ah, horses." The old man said contemplatively. And then he added with a shake of his head, "There are horses, but no man named Joe."

"But we're supposed to meet a man named Joe where the horses are," Grace clarified.

"Are you sure?" Alan reiterated apprehensively. "We are to meet him at the livery, where the horses are, on the north end of town, err, I mean village."

"I can take you, but no man named Joe there," the old man repeated with a mocking sarcasm.

"But can you take us to the horses anyway?" Grace interjected, getting a little impatient herself as to how the conversation was going.

"Okay, okay, this way," the old man directed, summoning with his hand and pointing to a path between two huts. "We go, but no man there," he insisted, doubtfully shaking his head at their persistence and mumbling something to himself in his native dialect.

As the party of adventurers approached the livery hut, where a few fenced-in horses grazed in a small corral, they noticed a young woman with long blond hair grooming one of the horses.

"Hello, there," Alan called out, getting the woman's attention and continuing to speak slowly. "We're looking for a guide named Joe from the Comoe National Park."

The woman turned and gazed curiously at the oddly dressed foreigners for a moment. With a suspicious look she then exclaimed, "No inglesa. Go way."

"No speak English?" Alan inquired.

"No inglesa," the woman reiterated, returning again to the care of her horse.

Seeing Alan was getting nowhere with this village woman, Grace's father turned inquisitively to the old man for help, sounding rather silly with his over-articulating. "Can - you - help – us? Ask - if - she - knows - Joe?"

The old man only shrugged his shoulders as he looked helplessly at the frustrated travelers. Now it was Grace's turn to try to communicate.

"Sir," Grace started indignantly, looking at the old man in frustration and caring very little how articulate she sounded. "Look here, it is very important that we find this Joe person as soon as possible!"

Just then a suppressed giggle, followed by an outburst of laughter came from behind the horse, as the old man in turn slapped his knee and doubled over in hysterical laughter. Still trying to compose herself, the blond woman stepped from behind the horse and offered her hand in greeting, first to Alan, then the others. "Hi, I'm Joe," the woman said playfully, with dancing eyes. "I'm sorry, but old Ty and I couldn't resist; it is how we greet all our foreign visitors when we get the chance. This is Ty, and welcome to the Ivory Coast."

"The gullible ones," Alan said, addressing Joe. "Why didn't you tell us in your emails that you were a woman?" Alan asked, with a grin that showed his embarrassment.

"What fun would that have been?" Joe answered back, with a teasing smile. "Besides, you didn't ask."

"So now what?" Jim asked, noticing Grace's understandable impatience to get moving to Dr. Clark's camp.

"We wait," Joe answered.

"Wait?" Grace questioned in surprise, already forming a dislike for their new guide.

"Yes," Joe said, pointing to the sky. "We don't move until that storm front is past. It will be hard enough to find our way through the jungle underbrush in good weather, but impossible, even for me, in a storm."

"How long do you think?" Alan inquired, seeing Grace's disappointment at the proposed delay.

"We should be on our way day after tomorrow, or the next, at the latest," Joe assured everyone. "In the meantime, we'll make good use of this time getting familiar with jungle life and learning woodcraft fundamentals."

"Woodcraft?" Jim asked, puzzled.

"It means wilderness or survival training," Alan chimed.

"Hey, Alan, you know your stuff, don't you?" Joe responded, looking at him admiringly.

"Alan's been quite the outdoorsman ever since . . . ah, well, for several years now, anyway." Grace's father stumbled over his words, realizing just in time that Alan alone had the right to divulge the personal reason for his self-imposed wilderness living of late.

"Since when?" Joe asked innocently.

"It's a long story," Alan answered, unprepared at the moment to venture into his personal life history with virtual strangers. "Perhaps another time."

"Yes, of course," Joe said, a little embarrassed, yet curious to know the mystery. She proceeded to lead them into a well-furnished hut near the livery.

Just then, an ear-shattering crash, followed by a loud thunderclap, shook everything around them, as a torrent of rain started pummeling the thatched roof above them.

"It is too bad about the policias taking your guns," Joe mentioned, using the distraction of the thunderstorm's onslaught to deflect from her innocent, though unwitting, faux pas. "I have new ones for you, though I'm sure not as nice as those you brought from America, but they will do in a pinch. I'll show them to you tomorrow."

"Any updates on the recent disturbances?" Grace asked, hoping nothing else would hinder their already delayed start.

"Nothing lately, but it's still a fluid situation. If I hear anything I'll let you know," Joe answered, trying to be as encouraging as the truth would allow.

"I noticed Ty left just as the storm broke," Grace's father observed. "Will he be going with us?"

"No," Joe answered; with a strange melancholy laugh that seemed more like a sigh. "No, Ty is getting too old for expeditions into the interior. He used to be my father's guide when I was younger, but still does a great job helping me out around here. He just left now to check on the mules; they get skittish in this kind of weather, and we need them healthy and rested for when we head out."

"You don't think the storm will delay us too long, do you?"

"I don't think so, Grace," Joe answered reassuringly. "We're still a good month out yet from the rainy season."

"What's next?" Alan asked, curious as to the details of the terrain and route they would be taking.

"Tomorrow I'll show you the map, the trail we'll be taking and the area where I think Dr. Clark's camp is . . ."

"You don't know where he is?" A surprised Jim interrupted, but not rudely.

"I thought you were the guide that took him to his current location?" Grace quickly commented, echoing Jim's astonishment.

"As you know, I did take Dr. Clark to a specific region in Ghana's Mole National Park, but he told me that his research might eventually take him elsewhere, maybe even miles from the original drop-off point," Joe explained calmly, sensing the heightened emotions and disappointment around her. "It's been almost a year, so he may have moved his camp several times by now."

Grace groaned at hearing this news. *First the hassle with the authorities upon arrival, then the storm, and now this,* she thought, lamenting the possibility of even more delays. Then sighing, she said, "I'm tired; I think I'll go to bed."

"That's a good idea. It's been a long day, and I think we could all use some sleep," Alan said sympathetically, not wanting Grace to feel singled out as the reason for breaking up the meeting.

Having prepared their bedding and mosquito netting earlier in the day, the exhausted and somewhat discouraged adventurers retired for the night, leery of what the next day might bring.

Over the next two days Joe reviewed the map with the crew, and with Alan's help, taught the basics of wilderness survival and communications.

"The jungle is full of white noise as you have already noticed. A constant chorus of insects, birds, monkey chatter, and so on is normal. What isn't normal is silence; this is one of the first clues of danger nearby. Be alert at all times, but especially if the jungle suddenly goes silent; it's a clear indication that danger is near," Joe warned.

For security she highlighted a specific area for each team member to observe while on the expedition. Joe would scan ahead to the front of the column, Jim the left, Grace the right and Alan was to oversee the entire caravan, as well as being designated the rear guard. Joe appointed Alan to this crucial position because of his keen eyes and extensive woodcraft experience.

During a break in the training, Ty brought up a mule with a couple of sacks on each side. Joe threw back a tarp and started handing out the replacement guns they had lost to the authorities.

"Like I said, these are not as nice as the ones you brought, but they'll kill a leaping lion or a charging buffalo just as well."

'Not as nice' was clearly an understatement, as Joe laid out the first few rifles for inspection.

It looks like they've just been salvaged from a civil war era museum, Alan thought, gazing upon the antiquated display of fire-arms. However, after target practice and sighting the rifles in, Alan warmed to their usefulness and gained a little more respect for their accuracy.

"They'll do," was his only comment to Joe as they packed them away for the night.

After target practice and sighting in their guns, Grace and her father hurried off to the communications hut for one last call home before leaving the next day; it likely would be several weeks before they were back in Tagati for another opportunity.

CHAPTER 5

Finding William C. Clark

Part 3: Alan and Joe's World

"IT SEEMS WE'VE BEEN left alone," Alan pointed out to Joe, with a hint of gladness in both his voice and eyes.

"So it seems," Joe responded with a similar shy twinkle in her own eyes, before looking down and hiding them under her long lashes. Then, remembering the look on Grace's anxious face as she hurried off to the communication hut, she initiated their conversation. "Do you think I offended Grace when you first arrived, Alan; I mean with my little prank with Ty?" Joe's tone was distinctly apologetic. "I didn't realize, I mean, if I had known the seriousness . . ."

"Don't give it another thought," Alan interrupted, assuring Joe there was nothing to be concerned about. "Grace is fine. Besides, she understands now that we couldn't have left until the storm passed anyway."

"Yes, I know, but now that I understand more clearly why she is so desperate to find Dr. Clark, I still feel bad."

"This has been a long, hard journey for Grace, but she's strong and determined," Alan said, in prideful admiration of his young friend.

"I can plainly see that," Joe agreed.

"About the other day, when Jim started to mention my past," Alan said, distracting Joe from any lingering guilt or embarrassment, and inviting her to sit down next to him. "If you're interested, I'd like to tell you about it. It's been a while since . . . well, since someone has interested me enough, well . . . you know."

Alan saw a crimson glow flush across Joe's face for an instant, with a shy tilt of her head again.

"I would be honored," Joe remarked, as she looked up at Alan, unable to hide her admiration. "You interest me as well; we have so much in common."

"We do," Alan agreed and then asked, "Ty said your parents were missionaries, and . . ."

"Oh no, no, you first," Joe interrupted, filled with curiosity, as she touched Alan's arm gently for emphasis. "What's the mystery? What's this deep, dark secret in your past that Jim almost spilled?"

"Oh, there's no big mystery really," Alan hesitated, "it's just, well . . ."

"Go ahead; I'm truly interested," Joe urged sincerely.

Alan began to explain how his first wife, Janet, had suffered for years through painful cancer treatments, eventually succumbing to its ravages, and dying just one month before his best friend, Paul.

At this point Joe, moved with compassion, placed her hand gently on his.

"Paul was more than a friend," Alan continued, appreciating Joe's simple gesture. "He was my mentor, helping me in those early years of my political career. His wife's name was Elle, and she and Janet were inseparable. You can imagine how hard it was to lose both so close together. Well, to make a long story short, Elle and I remained good friends, and a few years later were engaged to be married. However, something Gloria did changed everything in such a profound way; we couldn't have imagined it at the time."

Alan stopped, as he considered whether bringing Gloria into his narrative would betray a confidence. As Alan vacillated, Joe waited patiently for him to sort out whatever was going on in his mind. After a minute of silent deliberation however, he knew Gloria saw her past more as a witness of God's love and forgiveness than an embarrassment. He also realized that it was virtually impossible to unravel the next sequence of events without adding her into his storyline, so Alan resumed with some apprehension.

"Gloria, well, ah . . . regrettably, she had an abortion."

Joe, a missionary's daughter and brought up to respect all life, even that of the unborn, listened curiously as Alan continued.

"Although there were no serious physical complications, emotionally she fell apart. You see, a strange thing happened during the abortion; actually, a God thing. She had a dream, a dream about their life together; the child she was aborting, right up to her baby's wedding day! You can't imagine what it was like for her to wake up, only to find it was too late. She never did see her daughter, except in her dreams."

Alan proceeded to share how Gloria tried everything to relieve her conscience, and how her search for redemption and forgiveness made him rethink his own worldview. "You've probably heard us talk about Grace's little sister, Jeni—that was her name. Of course, if Jeni had lived, technically she would have been Grace's *older* sister. I suppose it's because she never had a chance to grow up that we affectionately still refer to her as Grace's *little* sister."

"That is so terribly sad," Joe remarked, tears welling up in her eyes. "What she must have gone through. And you, how heartbreaking to lose both your wife and friend at the same time."

"Thanks, Joe," Alan said appreciatively. Then, desiring to lighten the melancholy mood that was settling around them, abruptly asked, "By the way, your name isn't really Joe, is it?"

"No, of course not," Joe answered with a bashful giggle. "My parents named me Josephine, but it was too hard, or I should say, too inconvenient and cumbersome for the villagers to pronounce, so the nickname stuck. Actually, I was such a tomboy, it fit pretty well anyway. I can't remember the last time anyone called me by my real name. But please go on, I still don't see how Grace's little sister could have influenced so many lives. I'm very interested."

"Okay, *Josephine*," Alan said teasingly. "I'll continue."

"Oh, Alan!" Joe shot back, somewhat embarrassed at the unfamiliar sound of her name being spoken by another, while her feminine instincts did not miss Alan's veiled flirtation with that tease. She approved, and genuinely liked how her birth name sounded as Alan spoke it.

"You see," Alan said, getting back to his and Gloria's life stories, "at the time, Elle and I were both atheists, and as long as we shared that same worldview, everything was fine. My first doubts came when I saw the devastating effect of Gloria's abortion. It would have broken your heart to see her then. She tried everything to ease the pain and guilt. She tried drugs, therapy, the advice of friends, and even time, but nothing helped.

I remember how Elle sincerely tried to dissuade Gloria from her guilt by trying to convince her that Jeni was just a lifeless, meaningless cluster of cells, no different than a wart. She continued on to insist that it was her legal right. But to Gloria it was a big deal, because she knew her baby was alive, because she had experienced a heart-wrenching true-to-life relationship with her baby in her dream.

She became desperate. The feelings of guilt and regret continued to haunt her, until she sought help from a mutual Christian friend of ours, Frances. It was then, after seeing the miracle of Gloria's transformation from hopeless bitterness, despair and guilt, to finding forgiveness and peace through a simple relationship with Jesus Christ, that I saw the true power and reality of our living God! Joe, I had never seen anything like that before, and it changed me; I've never been the same since!"

Alan paused, reflecting for a moment, and then proceeded, "Romans 8:28 says, *and we know that all things work together for good to them that love God, to them who are called according to His purpose.* Everyone who knew Gloria and Jeni would attest to the pure truth of this scripture!"

"Wow," Joe responded enthusiastically, beginning to see how Jeni's brief life, even in her mother's womb, could make such a powerful impact for good. "So, you're saying that it was through Gloria and Jeni that you became a Christian and changed your entire worldview?"

"Yes, but not just me!" Alan said excitedly. "Gloria's mom, her husband Jim, Jim's parents, my parents, Grace, Piper, and so many others; not to mention the legislation I was able to push through before retiring, saving who knows how many lives; all due to Jeni, a little girl who supposedly never existed, by earthly standards that is!"

"How wonderful!" Joe lit up, as she started to get a full picture, through God's mercy and promise, of how an aborted little girl who never saw the light of day, could have influenced so many lives.

"After realizing the brutality and evils of abortion, it became one of my goals to help women see their child as a person, and just how much love and life they would miss if they went through with it. If women could experience life with their child like Gloria did before making that decision, it would make all the difference in the world!"

"It sure would!" Joe agreed wholeheartedly.

"Anyway," Alan said, getting back to his storyline, "it wasn't long before my new worldview and Elle's clashed, and clashed to the point where continuing our relationship was impossible."

"Then Elle wasn't one of the many people Jeni helped?"

"Sadly, no. She felt betrayed and rejected, eventually breaking off all communication with us."

"Where is she now—if you don't mind me asking?"

Alan hesitated, as it was a heartbreaking question to answer. Elle was a distant memory now, and not a pleasant one.

"She's gone," Alan answered somberly, averting his eyes from Joe's. "Elle started drinking soon after, heavily, and well . . . she was so angry and bitter, she never got over it. I tried to help, we all did, but she wouldn't have anything to do with us. Eventually . . . well, they said it was her liver."

"Alan, I'm so sorry," Joe empathized.

"That was several years ago now, but around that same time, my second wife Alice, was killed in a traffic accident."

"Oh no!" Joe gasped breathlessly, shocked and overwhelmed with compassion and grief, as Alan continued.

"And that's about it," Alan concluded, summing up the high and low points of his life to date. "After Alice passed, I needed to get away for a while to clear my head and spend some quality time alone with God. So, I resigned from politics and started backpacking through some of the most remote wilderness regions of the world, even the Amazon."

"But never the Ivory Coast?" Joe asked, with a subtle implication radiating from her eyes.

"No, although the Ivory Coast does remind me a little of the South American jungles, at least what I've seen of it so far," Alan answered, oblivious to Joe's own flirtatious hint.

"Grace is very fortunate to have someone with your experience and skill with her on this expedition," Joe said, and then building upon her previous 'implication', added, "And I'm so glad circumstances, as bad as they are, brought you here."

"I'd call it a divine appointment," Alan added, while in typical male fashion was slow to get the hint, but eventually getting there. "Joe, I'm glad we were brought together as well. I haven't allowed myself to be this vulnerable in a long time."

"I'll take that as a compliment," Joe responded with a radiant smile and a twinkle in her eyes, relieved to finally get her desired reaction from Alan.

"But enough about me," Alan said abruptly, feeling a little uncomfortable with the current level of sentimentality. "What's your story, Joe? Ty told me your parents were missionaries and died many years ago. What happened?"

"Alan, my parents didn't . . ." Joe hesitated, feeling the words more than speaking them. ". . . They didn't just die; they were brutally murdered by a cannibal tribe that lived near here at the time."

This time it was Alan's turn to place a compassionate hand on Joe's, as she went on to describe that fateful day.

"Thirty years ago . . ." Joe paused again, momentarily tormented by her stirred memories of that horrifying day, ". . . everything happened so fast. A civil war broke out, and we were in such a remote area, the consulate had no time to warn us. I was only sixteen at the time."

Joe welcomed a comforting arm around her, as she continued.

"Good old Ty was my parents' interpreter and guide to the outlying tribes. If it hadn't been for him, I would have been lost along with my parents. You see, those practicing the ancient arts of human sacrifice, cannibalism and Albino harvesting, were emboldened during the chaos and confusion at the onset of the war. They attacked small, isolated villages like ours throughout the region;

especially looking for white foreigners due to their high value on the black market. As you can imagine, in all the confusion the authorities were overwhelmed and lacked the resources to maintain civil control. Ty has been like a father to me ever since."

Albino harvesting? Alan thought, momentarily distracted by this strange new thing. He had learned much about the witch-doctors of east Africa and the cannibals of New Guinea, but had never heard of Albinos. Although very curious to learn about these mysterious Albinos and what Joe meant by `harvesters', he did not want to interrupt her narrative and chose to delay his curiosity for another time.

"Anyway," Joe went on, "I was in the living room doing homework, while Mom and Dad were working in the garden. All of a sudden I heard a terrifying cry from my mom, followed by my dad yelling at her to run. Instantly, there was screaming and confusion all around me. A second later, before I knew what had happened, Ty burst through the back door, grabbed me, and dragged me into the secret underground safe-room my dad had dug in case of such an emergency. We waited and waited, but my parents never came. As I grew older, I realized my parents didn't even try; if they had, they would have led them straight to our hiding place. Alan," she said, looking up into his eyes, "they gave their lives to save Ty and me!"

Alan listened quietly but intently, as Joe continued to unveil the tragic details of her parents' fate.

"All Ty and I could do was listen helplessly to the cries of my parents, and the other villagers above us. Then, those barbarians came into our house looking for me. I knew enough of their language to know they knew I was there, and they were determined to find me. They literally destroyed the house trying but never discovered our hiding place. Eventually they gave up, and an eerie silence followed. Even the jungle was silent, and in that moment I knew I would never see my parents again."

Joe looked away to hide her tears, while Alan affectionately and gently squeezed her small, trembling hand. They both sat in quiet reflection for several minutes, reverently honoring Joe's parents. Then, while drying her eyes, Joe turned and looked appreciatively at Alan. "We both have had our share of troubles, haven't we?"

"Yes, that's one thing I wish we didn't have in common," Alan mused solemnly; and then, seizing the opportunity the break in the conversation afforded, decided to satisfy his curiosity about the Albinos and harvesters.

"I'll tell you in a minute," Joe said, still drying her eyes. "But first, I'll freshen up a bit and get you more coffee."

Joe disappeared into the kitchen and returned a few minutes later with Alan's coffee, rejuvenated and looking like her old carefree self again.

Setting Alan's coffee on the table, she smiled and tossed her long blond hair back out of her face with a sweep of her hand. "There," she said, "I feel much better."

"So, Josephine," Alan asked, teasingly again, "what about those Albinos?"

This time Joe graciously accepted Alan's boyish flirtation without comment and liked how it sounded.

"The Albinos are a rare race of African natives with a genetic defect that causes the pigment of their skin to be white. Many of the local tribes refer to them as *Ghost People*, or the *Invisibles*. Many tribes, especially in this area of the Ivory Coast, are ignorant and superstitious, and they believe Albino hair and certain body parts have special healing attributes, as well as placebo powers, especially when harvested from younger Albinos, which is why very few Albinos reach adulthood. We hide as many as we can until we're able to move them to safer locations, but they are superstitious themselves, and fear white people almost as much as the harvesters."

"It's hard to believe such barbaric practices are still happening in this modern age."

"But they do," Joe volunteered with a shiver. "Even now, as you know, skirmishes between opposing political and tribal factions have increased almost daily in this region, not to mention that there is still a large demand on the black market, for . . . for what these harvesters provide."

"I know. I remember you warned us that there might be trouble before we came."

"I was hesitant to allow you to come at all, but, well, Grace was so insistent; I couldn't refuse. How is Piper doing?"

"We'll know more when Grace and her father return from the communication hut, but the last time I spoke with Frank, Grace's husband, I sensed an urgency in his voice that time was of the essence."

"I'm sure it is, Alan. This must be so hard on Grace; still, we couldn't have left right away. It's hard enough to maneuver these overgrown jungle trails in good weather, but nearly impossible in bad weather."

"I know, Joe, and don't feel at all responsible for any delay. We all know you're doing the best you can; you're the expert and know what's best."

"Well, our wait is over now," Joe said with a relieved sigh. "Tomorrow we start."

"Where's Grace?" Alan asked, as Jim returned from the communication hut without her.

"The news wasn't good," Jim answered with red swollen eyes. "She wanted to be alone. I'm afraid we're running out of time."

CHAPTER 6

Finding William C. Clark

Part 4: Into the Jungle

TEMPORARILY ON LOAN FROM the Comoe National Park as one of the most experienced Africa Tour Operators in the service, Joe was highly recommended for this specific duty. Joe and Ty had everything flawlessly organized and ready to go the next morning, with two mules heavily laden with equipment and supplies needed for their journey. Joe had hired two strong local villagers, Yaya and Siaka, who also attended Joe's Bible Study, to assist with guiding the pack mules, trailblazing, setting up camp and other general duties, including security. The weather was finally cooperating, with the morning sun shimmering bright in the east through the Iroko trees.

"Now, before we get started," Joe warned, after morning prayers and Bible reading, "one of the most important things to remember is that if there's anything or anyone out there laying in wait to attack us, we will never hear it; if we do, it will probably be too late. So, keep your eyes alert at all times in your designated areas. Also, every once in a while look to your neighbor; a teammate looking out for you will see trouble before you do a high percentage of the time."

After days of anxious waiting, Grace was relieved they had finally started their excursion into the jungle. Yaya led the way, clearing the trail as necessary. Siaka was close behind, leading the mules as the caravan started for a wide clearing on the northeast side of the village. The trail was well worn nearer the village for the first several miles, leaving plenty of room between the broad leaves, vines and gnarly trees. However, as they ventured further into the jungle, the well-worn path began to narrow; encroaching on either side, as unconsciously every eye and ear began to scrutinize the slightest noise or movement around them.

"Wait!" Joe cried out intensely, but softly and quickly raised a hand for the processional to stop. The jungle had become deathly quiet, as Joe pointed two fingers to her eyes and then waved a hand around her, gesturing for the team to keep a vigilant lookout. The forest was still, just as Joe had warned, as each set of eyes scanned in every direction for danger. A few minutes later, however, they started to hear a jostling of branches and chattering noises high above them. When they looked up, several monkeys and birds were again jumping from branch to branch. Soon, the trees and dark haze of dense foliage were again engulfed in the familiar white noise of clamoring animals, birds and insects.

"It's okay now," Joe said, to everyone's relief. "Whatever it was is gone."

"What was it?" Grace asked, turning to Joe, clearly unnerved a little by their first brush with danger.

"I'm not sure. It could have been anything, though I don't think it was human; they're not so easily spooked."

The caravan moved on slower now, and much more warily after this first frightening encounter with an unknown nemesis; but as the day went on without incident, they started to relax again and move at a steady pace.

Suddenly a loud shot was heard from behind them, quickly followed by another – bang, bang! Everyone unconsciously dropped to the ground. Grace shrieked in horror, as a heavy, furry object blackening the sky above her, knocked her to the ground with a crushing blow and a loud thud. Dazed for a moment, she looked up to see a wide gaping mouth of a spotted golden leopard, with its long white fangs just inches from her face, motionless, and struggling to breathe. Grace involuntarily let out a scream of revulsion as she struggled to scramble out from under the heavy dying beast.

"Is everyone alight?" Alan yelled, running to Grace's side, with smoke still filtering from the muzzle of his antiquated gun.

"Not my nerves," Grace admitted, still struggling to extricate herself from under the beast, as Alan reached down to help.

Joe quickly thrust a knife between the creature's ribs to make certain the beast was no longer a threat, as Grace's father ran to his terrified daughter to make sure she was al- right.

"Where did it come from?" Jim asked, as he gazed up into the trees. "There are no branches up there strong enough to hold the weight of a cat this size."

"That's because it didn't come from up there," Joe corrected. "Leopards are stalkers. They quietly creep low to the ground and then spring on their prey from an advantageous position."

"Well, where did it come from then?" Grace asked, confused. "It seemed to fall from the sky right on top of me!"

"Alan can answer that," Joe said, looking at Alan in admiration. "That was quite a shot."

Tipping his hat in recognition of Joe's compliment, Alan turned to Grace.

"A leopard can jump as far as eighteen feet, and as high as ten," Alan explained. "I could barely see it slowly moving toward you, crouching behind those Elephant Ear plants and Tree Ferns, about twenty feet away. So, I had to wait until it lunged at you before I could get a clear shot. He was all of ten feet in the air when I hit him with the first one."

"That's why it looked like it fell from the trees," Joe added matter-of-factly, being no stranger to this sort of event. "Alan shot the leopard in mid-air, as it was lunging for the attack."

Grace tried to speak, but she couldn't form a word. Her knees buckled from the delayed reaction of the shock; Jim caught her just before she hit the ground. He lowered her gently the rest of the way to rest and recover her nerves.

"That leopard was probably what was stalking us earlier, when our sudden movements spooked him," Joe commented later. "It must have been tracking us all day, looking for another opportunity to strike."

"What now?" Grace's father asked.

"What now is we will have to dress it, take it with us, and report it to the game commission when we get back. It doesn't have a tag, so that's good; it will save me a lot of paperwork."

"Sorry about that," Alan said, wondering if he had done something wrong, or even illegal, by shooting the leopard.

"It's never wrong to save a human life at the expense of an animal's," Joe answered sadly. "It's just tragic when it's necessary."

Days are short in the jungle with the thick foliage of the trees above blocking the sunlight, speeding the arrival of nighttime, so Joe suggested that they make camp for the night. This would also give Yaya and Siaka some extra time to clear a heavier than usual amount of underbrush up ahead before turning in.

When Grace wearily rested her head on her pillow under the mosquito netting that night, she wasn't laughing; she was terrified, and wondered if she could even go on. She knew for her own sake she wouldn't have given it another thought, but this trial and testing of a mother's love wasn't for her, *This is for you, Piper*, she repeated over and over as she fell asleep that night . . . *this is for you . . .*

CHAPTER 7

Finding William C. Clark

Part 5: Unexpected Disaster

SLEEPING IN THE JUNGLE is not for the faint of heart, especially the first night; and especially if the day before you were only a second away from being mauled by an attacking leopard. So, it wasn't surprising that Jim, and Grace in particular, were far from refreshed and rested the next morning, a rest they would soon deeply regret not having.

"Jefa! Jefa, Joe! Escucha! " Siaka yelled excitedly, running with Yaya up to Joe, after just a few hours of breaking camp. The others saw Siaka and Yaya speaking intensely and with flailing arms, pointing to the path ahead.

"What do you think it is, Alan," Grace's father asked, as they all huddled together, keeping a sharp eye out for trouble.

"Escucha, is French for listen," Grace interpreted, "but he's talking so fast, it's hard to make out what else he's saying; something about drums and turning back I think."

"That doesn't sound good, "Alan said, as Joe motioned everyone to be quiet.

Joe listened intently for a few minutes, and then turned to the trio of curious onlookers.

"Well, it begins; they know we're here," Joe said, walking up to the anxious group. "I was hoping to avoid this, but I knew it was a possibility."

"Avoid what?" Grace asked with trepidation.

"A war tribe called the Yakuba," Joe answered. "If you listen closely, you can hear their communication drums. I heard there was a warring faction that had migrated to the east, claiming ancestral rights to the mountainous regions northwest of us, but we have been heading northeast, so I was sure we would not encounter them."

"Are you still sure?" Grace gasped.

"The drums don't lie." Joe answered with a concerned sigh. "Just another development to make our trip a little more interesting and challenging."

"But Yaya and Siaka seemed extremely frightened and excited just now, and they said something about turning back," Jim commented anxiously.

"So Grace, you know a little French, I see," Joe said with admiration. "I'm impressed."

"But what about the Yakuba?" Grace insisted.

"Yes," Alan inquired. "Yaya and Siaka seem petrified at hearing the drums!"

"Don't mind them," Joe answered, unconcerned. "They are very superstitious and have been told from childhood about the ancient myths of the bloodthirsty Yakuba. And, although the Yakuba still wear the same traditional paint and beads of their warrior ancestors, if we continue in a northeasterly direction, they won't feel threatened and will probably leave us alone."

"Probably?" Grace asked, unconvinced of their safety.

"Like I said, it will add another element of intrigue to our little adventure, but I'm confident we can move forward in safety. You don't want to turn back now, do you?"

"No . . ." Grace answered reluctantly, wishing there was any other way to save Piper.

"What about Yaya and Siaka?" Jim asked.

"Unfortunately, I had to double their salary to keep them with us," Joe said regrettably, shrugging her shoulders. "C'est la vie! We move on."

True to Joe's word, the Yakuba were all bark and no bite, at least for the present. And although the incessant pounding of the drums weighed heavily on their nerves, within a day's march, had faded away into the distance.

After that unnerving experience, the team finally had a few days of quiet traveling, enjoyed some exquisite mountain views, herds of buffalo and elephants meandering through the great plains of open prairies, and even a family of hippopotami frolicking in a river eddy from a bluff a hundred feet below them; until one morning . . .

"Alan, wake up. Everyone up!" A worried-looking Joe roused the group, long before daybreak.

"What is it?" Grace asked, rubbing the sleep from her eyes. "More drums?"

"No, worse!" Joe answered with obvious concern on her face, "Thunder."

"Thunder?" Alan questioned alertly, looking at Joe's intense eyes.

"Yes, thunder, and we need to make a decision now. Do we secure camp and hold out for a day or two, or break camp immediately and take our chances moving on in the storm."

"Joe, we've already lost over two days from the last storm!" Grace said excitedly, not thinking of the danger that could be ahead if they pressed on.

"But, Grace," Grace's father scolded, "what if we get lost in the storm or worse?"

"I don't understand, Joe," Alan asked, confused. "The weather report said we had clear skies all week!"

"Alan, listen to the direction of the thunder; it's to the east," Joe responded, knowing Alan would get the hint.

"Ah, a mountain thunderhead," Alan groaned.

"Yes, a mountain-driven storm; rare, but they do happen on occasion this time of year," Joe explained. "It likely won't be as bad as the last one, but I still don't recommend trying to traverse it in the dense area of the jungle that we are currently in."

"But you're not absolutely against continuing?" Grace questioned hopefully.

"That's why this needs to be a team decision; I cannot take full responsibility if we continue," Joe stressed.

"The last report on Piper's condition was desperate," Jim said, indicating his leaning on the subject.

"For Piper's sake, I don't see how we can waste another minute," Grace agreed.

"Well, this quest has been for Piper from the beginning," Alan nodded in agreement. "It's our safety against her life; I say we move."

"Then it's agreed. Let's break camp as quickly as we can and get moving," Joe commanded.

After the meeting Yaya and Siaka had another heated and animated discussion with Joe, mixing several of their native dialects with French and even a few words of English. They felt this excursion had had enough excitement already, and were ready to turn back. It wasn't long, however, that Joe again had persuaded them to continue, mostly by appealing to their egos, calling them little children; cowards in their culture. So, with much grumbling and complaining under their breath, Yaya and Siaka reluctantly returned to their places in front of the mules and led on.

"Look there," Grace noticed later that morning, pointing to several birds circling above them to the north.

"Vultures," Alan suggested.

"Yes, vultures waiting for some poor creature to die, or to become weak enough not to threaten their mid-day snack," Joe explained.

"How awful," Grace gasped with a shiver, but the spectacle was soon forgotten, due to the darkening skies above.

In spite of the looming threat above them, the first few hours had been mercifully uneventful, as they were making relatively good time on a wider and less overgrown part of the trail; that is, until the expected deluge of rain hit with a crushing blow. The already dark forest descended quickly into a midnight blackness, as the accompanying lightning crashed ever closer.

"What now, Joe?" Alan yelled, knowing that hearing him would be difficult over the deafening swirl of the wind and rain now pummeling the caravan.

"I'll take point!" Joe shot back with a hand cupped to her mouth, "Bring everyone up close. No need for lookouts in this weather; pass it on!"

The time they had gained had now been lost, as every foot of advance was painstakingly slow, not to mention very uncomfortable. The thick, wet jungle seemed to swallow them up, as they moved deeper and deeper into the darkness.

"Halt!" Joe suddenly cried out, putting up a hand.

Only Yaya and Siaka up front with the mules were able to hear or see her command through the noise and blinding rain of the violent tempest. As the caravan came to an abrupt stop, Alan made his way to Joe to find out what had happened.

"No more trail," Joe yelled in frustration, seeing Alan approach and knowing his mission. "Look!"

Before them rushed a raging torrent of water; an angry river swelled by the unexpected storm.

"I must have inadvertently turned down one of the path's tributaries," Joe yelled above the noise of the storm, quite upset with herself for such a blunder.

"How could it have been helped in this weather," Alan yelled back, attempting to put a Band-Aid on Joe's bruised ego. "What now?"

"Everyone stay here, while I backtrack to find where I veered off the main path. I'll be back soon!"

Joe quickly disappeared out of sight into the storm, while Alan reported to the others what had happened and where she was going.

Grace's patience was wearing thin with all the delays, but she knew there was really no one to blame. Life was full of storms, whether real or imagined, and they had to be endured - but not alone. Grace had her faith, a faith stronger than any storm, stronger than life itself, and knew she could bear anything with that faith.

Joe finally returned to the wind-weary, rain-soaked travelers in just over an hour.

"I found the main road a few miles back, but it's too late to turn back now," Joe yelled above the ongoing fury of the storm. "We'll camp here for the night, and do the best we can under the circumstances. Then we'll start again in the morning. The storm probably will have let up by then!"

The storm had indeed cleared up by daybreak as Joe predicted, and they quickly stowed their makeshift camp for fast travel. They were all very grateful for the stark contrast of the current clear, blue sky, to the ominous dark clouds from the night before. The beauty of the morning rays of light now danced and shimmered through the tall, gnarly jungle trees into a thick, swirling mist caused by the previous night's rain. And, with their clothes quickly drying in the warm rays of that early morning sunlight, the group made their way back to the main trail, with the sound of the river's raging torrent of angry water slowly fading in the distance behind them. With the brightness of this new day, they were filled with hope for a better day's progress ahead. However, what looked to be a promising day of good weather and rapid pace would soon become their worst nightmare, tragically amplified by an unforeseen and unbelievably shocking betrayal.

CHAPTER 8

Finding William C. Clark

Part 6: Betrayed

ONCE ON THE MAIN trail again, Joe decided to stay on point due to the trail's heavy overgrowth.

"I can see how Joe lost her way so easily yesterday afternoon," Grace commented to her father, observing how hard it was to see the trail even in the clear light of day.

"She's probably the best there is within a thousand miles," Alan added, as they moved slowly behind the narrow passage Siaka and Yaya were blazing.

Eventually the narrow, overgrown path widened into a comfortable thoroughfare, much to the relief of the weary and worn travelers.

"Why are we slowing down?" Grace yelled to Joe, as the mules stopped suddenly.

But instead of answering, Joe dashed toward thick underbrush and disappeared. Moments later, piercing cries of what seemed like a hundred men were heard all round them, as drums began accompanying their guttural chants. Then, to everyone's horror, half naked savages wearing grotesque wooden masks and covered from head-to-toe in skeletal white war paint suddenly appeared one by one from the jungle on every quarter.

"What does this mean?" Terrified, Grace asked her dad. "Where did Joe go?"

"Be quiet, and don't move!" Alan insisted as the five remaining members of the team huddled together near one of the mules.

They were quickly surrounded. More than thirty natives with spears pulsating to the beat of the drums and drawn back in attack position were slowly tightening the circle around them, while chanting feverishly to the drums.

"Not stay—must run!" With eyes bulging in fear, Yaya screamed in broken English and started to break from the others in a dash.

"No, Yaya, wait!" Alan yelled, trying to grab him, but it was too late. Instantly the drums stopped as every native stood quiet and still. Seconds later a spear from out of nowhere pierced Yaya through the back. He instantly tumbled to the ground. Grace let out a scream at the brutal sight and fainted into Alan's arms. Then, as quickly as the eerie silence commenced, the menacing wild dancing and chanting resumed to the cadence of the drums. Thrusting their long spears forward and back and forth, as if to throw them at any second, the natives again moved closer to their shocked and helpless prisoners.

"Be still and stay calm." Alan instructed, with a gesture of his hand. "It appears they will only harm us if we run or act in a hostile way."

After several more minutes of celebration, everything became quiet again, as one of the natives approached them, taller, and dressed even more hideous than the others.

"Armes vers le bas! Vers le bas!" The native who appeared to be the leader yelled in French.

"Weapons down! Down!" Grace interpreted, now revived somewhat from her collapse.

"Armes Vers le bas!" he repeated, this time stepping forward and drawing back his spear a little higher with intensity.

Knowing a few guns against so many natives, even with inferior weapons, was hopeless; Alan started to lower his weapon, while giving a glance to the others to do the same. Immediately they were seized upon and had their hands tied behind their backs.

"Me, Kuuku," the clan leader said, pounding his chest. "No problemes ou de a jouer!"

"No trouble or die," Grace interpreted, while she tried to control her trembling.

With a short stroke of Kuuku's hand, the natives immediately lined up in single file and started marching forward down the same path Joe and the others had just traveled.

Alan noticed one of the natives pull his spear out of Yaya's back, and then rejoin the ranks.

"It could be worse," Alan whispered to Jim, noting the natives were leaving Yaya's body behind.

"How so?" Jim asked.

"If they were cannibals or headhunters, they would have taken his body."

"Silence!" Kuuku warned, administering a hard blow to Alan's back with the butt of his spear, causing Alan to double over in pain. He stumbled for an instant, and then clumsily regained his footing.

They traveled for about two hours, before reaching Kuuku's camp located in a clearing with mountains hovering over them in the distance. Then, the celebration resumed in earnest, more wild and hideous than ever. Four sturdy stakes about five feet apart, were quickly buried several feet into the soft jungle soil in a semi-circle around a pile of faggots and logs, as the four terrified captives had their hands and feet bound securely to each. A fire was soon ablaze in front of them, as the grotesque looking savages, with drums pounding, continued their wild, hideous dancing late into the night. They taunted their helpless captives mercilessly, thrusting spears into their faces, sometimes grazing their skin and drawing blood. Eventually, however, to the great relief of the captives, the taunting stopped, and the camp slowly quieted for the night.

Frank was right after all, Grace thought, as tears of fear and sadness trickled through the dirt and sweat clinging to her cheeks. *What have I done? Piper will be lost, and Frank will be all alone, just as he feared.* Resigned to the fact that this was the end, Grace second-guessed the reasonableness of this attempt to save Piper's life, and realized the practical common sense of Frank's argument against this venture. *But how could I have known, or even suspected, that in this modern age something like this was even possible? And then there's Joe*, she thought, with a rage only the severity of the current circumstances could have fostered in such a kind and loving heart; *running off like a coward to save her own skin!*

With their prey secure and well-guarded with two sentries posted about ten paces away on either side, the natives finally gave their captives the opportunity to communicate freely amongst themselves.

"Is everyone alright?" Alan was the first to speak, with only the flashing illuminations of the bonfire offering light.

There was a general consensus in the affirmative, though each voice was filled with trepidation as to what was to come the following day.

"How could Joe have betrayed us like this?" Grace groaned to no one in particular.

Alan was obviously disappointed. Although they had only known each other a short time, he couldn't believe that Joe was capable of such a cowardly action. Until what seemed to him to be a very selfish act on Joe's part, he even went so far in his mind as to imagine a possible future together. "I can't believe it," he eventually answered, with his thoughts belying his own words.

"What do you think our chances are, Alan?" Jim asked, trying to be brave for his daughter's sake.

"To be honest," Alan answered, seeing no need to build up false hope in a state of affairs obvious to all, "not very good."

So as not to alarm the others, Alan mentally reasoned which class of barbarians from Joe's descriptions this could be. He had already ruled out cannibals or headhunters as a possibility, because of their indifference to Yaya's body. That left Albino or white-skin harvesters as the most likely.

"Gardes partis," Siaka whispered to Grace, who was the nearest to him, after hearing a scuffling noise behind him. Astonished, she looked curiously both ways.

"Alan, the guards are gone. What could it mean?"

Suddenly, a familiar voice from the jungle undergrowth about ten yards behind them spoke in a quiet whisper. "On your lives, do not look around! Continue to act as though I'm not here."

Hope surged through each terror-filled captive as they recognized Joe's voice.

"I had to wait until the fire died down a little to take advantage of the darkness," Joe continued to whisper intently. "Listen carefully: I will come behind each of you and cut loose your bonds, but do not move. Stay in your positions as though still bound, until I give you the word. When I say 'go,' run toward my voice as quickly and quietly as you can into the underbrush. Stay together, and don't stop running until you hear from me! I will catch up with you as soon as I am able."

Smeared with the rich dark jungle soil to camouflage her appearance and hide her movements, Joe quietly cut all the leather cords binding her friends. Then, after looking around and scrutinizing the entire area, she carefully and silently gave the command.

On her signal every person turned as one and ran quietly into the jungle, with Alan in the lead and Joe observing every movement of the natives to see if their escape had been observed. Convinced there was no immediate danger of pursuit, Joe made her way into the jungle. Within a quarter of an hour however, they heard the beating of drums, as Kuuku's camp came alive with that same hideous uproar of drums and howling chants.

"No matter what happens," Joe instructed, catching up with the others, "Keep moving in the direction of the moon, to the east! I'm going to fall back to keep our flank secure!"

With that quick word of instruction, Joe disappeared again into the thick underbrush, but this time no one doubted her motive. Grace rebuked herself sharply for thinking such enmity toward someone who had become her friend, but only for an instant; regrets would have to wait. Survival was the first order of business, as she closely followed Alan through the black night, deeper and deeper into the jungle. They no longer feared the unknown dangers that might be lurking in the shadows around them, as they struggled and stumbled through the dense ferns and leafy undergrowth. Their only concern now was the known menace in hot pursuit behind them.

No people were better skilled in woodcraft than the hostile clans of the African jungles, so Joe knew that trying to hide was out of the question. She also knew that rescuing her friends might have only delayed the inevitable, as these jungle trackers were both skilled and relentless; but this she kept to herself. At that moment she knew hope was their best weapon of survival.

After hours of running through the endless obstacles of nature and fighting the elements, Joe rejoined the party. She encouraged them all to take a quick break, noticing how exhausted everyone was, and that if they didn't get some rest soon, they would collapse entirely and hopelessly fall back into the hands of their pursuers.

"We can only stop for a minute," Joe warned. "Kuuku's warrior scouts are everywhere, though the main body is still miles behind us."

"I don't think... I can go on," Grace said, exhausted and barely able to speak from breathlessness.

"We don't have a choice, Grace," Joe insisted, knowing the danger. "It's either run - or die!"

Just then they heard a twig snap and a swooshing sound break through the quiet night air, as Alan leaped between Grace and the sharp point of a spear. Alan let out a painful cry as he fell to the ground. Joe turned in an instant, and with a quick flick of her wrist, buried a knife deep into the throat of the savage that launched the deadly projectile.

"Alan!" Grace screamed, seeing the spear protruding from his chest.

"Let me look at him!" Joe insisted, dropping by his side. She noticed immediately the wound was fatal, though he was still conscious as she laid his head gently on her lap.

CHAPTER 9

Finding William C. Clark

Part 7: William C. Clark's World

BORN AND RAISED IN a Canadian coastal town, William C. Clark was a genius in his own right, and, like Grace, a very successful medical scientist. Early in his career, he and his wife May lost their son, Edmond C. Clark, to a rare disease. William worked desperately for months on developing a cure for this illness, but to no avail.

Dr. Clark knew that research and development to discover cures of rare diseases was very expensive, with little to no profit, so most institutions, research grants and advanced scientific studies invested little time and resources in these efforts. However, due to the deep and painful grief over the loss of their son, Dr. Clark committed the rest of his life and career to that very endeavor.

To date he had successfully discovered several plant-based cures, and was now over a hundred miles deep in the jungles of Africa working on another. Dr. Clark was stubborn, and once inspired was so deeply passionate and committed to his research, almost nothing could distract him from that goal. This is what Frank and Grace were up against, and why there was doubt Dr. Clark could be persuaded to deviate even a few days from his work. But having exhausted every other option, and with time running out for Piper, they saw no alternative.

After almost a year in the jungle, Dr. Clark was continuing to study the unique properties of a rare plant known as the African Teak (Pericopsis elata), believed to be the secret to formulating his latest cure. Listed as an endangered species, this rare plant was only known to grow in the Mole National Park region of Ghana, and was also known as the Afromosia Plant.

It took Dr. Clark almost two years of endless paperwork and red tape merely to be allowed to study this rare plant, even in very small quantities and under strict supervision.

Finally, however, after navigating through the international and local maze of bureaucratic red-tape, he received permission to study the plant in its natural habitation only. An entourage of support staff and a large security detail, initially thought unnecessary by Dr. Clark, set up camp on the western edge of the Mole National Park.

"It was tenuous work to get approval for our research, Tahu, but look at the results!" Dr. Clark said, motioning his highly educated native assistant over to one of the many scientific pieces of equipment that populated his laboratory. "It has all been worth it. Look here . . ."

Tahu, a graduate of the University of Nairobi, in the eastern African nation of Kenya, was not only a competent researcher himself, but was also instrumental in helping Dr. Clark secure permission to acquire samples of the African Teak for study.

"This looks good," Tahu responded, after peering into a microscope for a minute. "Looks stable."

"Yes, it does, Tahu," Dr. Clark explained without emotion, as though reading through a shopping list. "After repeated tests, there has been no variation in the result; it has been consistent."

"This means we can start animal trials soon!" Tahu responded excitedly, in stark contrast to his colleague's reaction.

"It does," Dr. Clark answered with a sigh of relief. "I think this is it!"

To Dr. Clark's great satisfaction, this indeed was it; he was less than two months away from taking the samples and research back to the States for final human trials.

Chief, bwana! Chief bwana!" A breathless sentry named Tama yelled, barging into Dr. Clark's tent, throwing back the canvas door. "Hayati say white bone devils capture white people up river!"

While waiting for his opportunity to set up camp in West Africa, Dr. Clark had done his homework, studying the ancient superstitious rituals of Albino harvesting, Cannibalism and the resurgence of human sacrificing in some of the regions around where he would be working. Although there had been a revival of these superstitions recently, he felt relatively safe, as these clans were hundreds of miles west. Hayati's description of this white skeletal-clad tribe however, made his blood run cold, as he had run across an article on this specific clan, one of the most ruthless of them all. Until now, Dr. Clark had felt fairly secure and had earned the respect of the more docile tribes in the region. His ability to diagnose and treat the most common illnesses made him an honored hero to all who knew him. However, Kuuku and his people knew nothing about Dr. Clark's benevolence, and probably wouldn't care if they had.

"Where's Hayati, Tama?" Dr. Clark demanded.

"Gathering troops, Chief bwana!"

"Good, we have no time to lose! This is bad. Secure a detail to guard the compound; I'll go with Hayati."

"Yes, Chief bwana! Right away!"

"Tahu, you stay here and help Tama secure the compound. These white people must be the American lady and her team I told you about. Hayati and I must hurry if this is indeed Kuuku and his devils. He'll be sacrificing them at first light if we don't get there in time."

CHAPTER 10

Finding William C. Clark

Part 8: Rescued Too Late

ALAN AND JOE'S EYES met, as Alan, forcing a tender smile through the pain, struggled to raise an affectionate hand to Joe's dirty, black-camouflaged face. He tenderly caressed Joe's cheek, but only for a moment, as his strength failed, and his arm fell limply back to the ground.

"Run!" Alan groaned weakly, wincing from the pain and peering longingly into Joe's swollen, tear-filled eyes. Joe was still holding his head lovingly in her lap, while tenderly running her fingers through his hair, reluctant to leave. "Run!" Alan earnestly pleaded again, "Before it's too late!"

"Alan, we can't just leave you here," Jim said, not realizing how hopeless his condition was.

"Alan, why did you do it?" Grace cried, overwhelmed with grief.

"I promised . . ." Alan started to speak; his words interrupted by a cough and an issue of blood trickling from the corner of his mouth. "I promised your mother . . ." he coughed again, as more blood streamed down his cheek, ". . . with my . . ."

Alan slowly closed his eyes for the last time, as Joe wept over him and placed a tender kiss on his forehead. Their anguish and shock were unbearable.

"Joe, we need to go!" Jim insisted, in spite of his own enormous grief, knowing there was still an immense danger around them. He knew grieving would need to wait, or there would be no one left to grieve for Alan, at least in Africa.

"Yes," Joe said, laying Alan's still head gently to the ground and getting up slowly. But it was too late; the sound of approaching footsteps surrounded them.

"Tu ne cours pas!" One of the natives shouted behind them, as another advanced, flexing his arm to launch his spear.

"Arret! Arret! No kill!" Another native ordered. "Kuuku say no kill!"

Captured again, they were bound and led back to Kuuku's camp, under a dreary morning light that was just beginning to gray the eastern sky. It had been a long night, actually a long day and night, with little sleep, food or water; they were depressed, discouraged, heart-broken and exhausted.

A plethora of tangled and confused thoughts overwhelmed Joe's mind, as she followed robotically step by step behind Siaka. Her head was bowed low in grief and humiliation. *How could this have happened?* She privately mourned Alan's loss, as a flood of tears streamed down her face, washing away in streaks the black camouflage and revealing the white, weatherworn and swollen skin beneath. Joe was proud and honorable, refusing to place blame on anyone else for her lack of judgment, even in her mind.

What could I have done differently? she lamented in self-reproach. *What an idiot I am! How could I have allowed this to happen? Oh, Alan . . .* Distracted by the fresh memory of Alan's fading life in her arms, Joe stumbled over a protruding root and fell hard to the ground.

"Leve-toi!" A native commanded, striking her in the ribs with the side of his spear, "Leve-toi!"

Jolted from her melancholy and self-pity, Joe struggled immediately to her feet, so as to not endure another painful spear-thrust by the native.

Underway again, the prisoners were on the march, each step bringing them closer to an unknown fate. Each grieved silently for his fallen friend. Love had never been spoken between Joe and

Alan; nevertheless, Joe felt the sting of its power in her heart. Alan had become more than an acquaintance, more than a friend; she saw it in his eyes as he lay dying on her lap. A budding hope of love, cut down before it had a chance to blossom. She wept bitterly at the thought of what might have been, adding another layer of sorrow to her already bitter self-reproach.

"Yaya, my friend," Siaka said quietly, looking back over his shoulder with tears in his eyes.

"I know," Joe said sorrowfully. "It was all my fault."

"No, Amante Lady . . ." Siaka started to protest, as he unexpectedly doubled over from pain.

"Silence, ou mourir!"

This time it was Siaka's turn to be silenced by the butt end of a spear, as his knees buckled, sending him to the ground.

"Listen . . ." Grace whispered into Joe's ear, moving up a little closer while the guards were distracted by Siaka's tumble to the ground.

"Gunfire!" Joe answered, now fully awakened from her inward, self-reproaching stupor.

As the ill-fated prisoners listened, more shots were heard in the distance and were getting closer. Then, without warning, the half-dozen or so natives guarding them disappeared quickly into the jungle toward the direction of the gunfire, leaving them alone.

"Siaka! Hands, quickly!" Joe motioned with her eyes, as Joe turned back to back with Siaka, allowing him to loosen her bonds.

"What can this mean?" Jim asked, as Joe's hands were loosed behind her.

"White people," Joe answered. "No clan, even Kuuku has no firearms like that. It has to be white people!"

Once they had all been loosed from their restraints, they apprehensively huddled together under the coldness of the night sky, wide-eyed, waiting anxiously for what would happen next. Exhausted and famished, they knew there was no hope of escape, even though free to run if they chose. No, they would wait and soon know their fate. Terrified yet hopeful, they waited as the gunfire eventually died down, and the jungle became silent again. *What next*, they thought helplessly, as they heard a distant trampling of footsteps making their way closer and closer through the thick jungle underbrush.

Then, "Hello!" A voice called out through the thick blackness. A British voice, with a distinct French/American accent. "Anyone there? Hello!"

"Over here! Over here!" A shout of elation rang out, as the four liberated prisoners jumped for joy, waving their arms wildly over their heads. The clear and unmistakably English greeting hailing them was an answer to their prayers.

A few seconds later several men in civilized apparel, along with a few natives also dressed curiously in western wear, emerged from the jungle with one of their previous captors reluctantly guiding them to their location.

"We're saved! Saved," is all they could say, hugging each other as their rescuers approached.

"Who are you, and where did you come from?" Grace asked, as a tall, wiry man with thick-lensed glasses and wearing khaki's and a bush hat, approached them with a hand of greeting.

"You must be Grace," the kindly man remarked with a smile and a firm handgrip. "Hi, Joe, Siaka," he acknowledged the two familiar faces.

"I'm Dr. Clark, as you've probably guessed by now, and behind me are some of my associates."

"Hi, Dr. Clark, this is Grace, her father Jim, and Siaka, whom I think you already know." Joe said, shaking his hand and introducing the team.

"We lost two just before you arrived," Joe said regretfully, "Yaya, Siaka's friend, and Alan, a dear friend of Grace and Jim's."

"I'm so sorry to hear that," Dr. Clark answered with a sympathy that was clearly genuine. "We came as quickly as we could, I'm truly sorry we didn't arrive sooner, or . . ."

"You're here now," Grace interrupted with grateful appreciation. "We might have all been lost, if you hadn't arrived when you did! We are very grateful."

As these greetings were being made, Dr. Clark's staff distributed food and administered first-aid as needed, while he suggested they rest an hour or so to recoup their strength before heading back.

Now safely under the watchful eye of Dr. Clark and his men, emotions that had been suppressed for survival's sake gave way; tears of grief for Alan and Yaya flowed freely.

"Well, it's time we should be shoving off," Dr. Clark suggested reluctantly. Not wanting to be insensitive, but clearly uncomfortable with the vulnerability of their current location, knowing that if any of Kuuku's men had escaped in the dark, they might return to avenge their Chief.

As they were on their way Dr. Clark explained how he had learned of their capture through his head scout Hayati, and how he knew their situation was desperate from the description of the dreadful skeletal war paint and grotesque wooden masks.

"I had no idea that Kuuku and his resurrected Denkyira clan had migrated this far East," Dr. Clark commented in surprise.

"We didn't either. They were last reported to be west of the Comoe, over three hundred miles away!" Joe lamented, equally surprised.

"You couldn't have known," Dr. Clark said consolingly, noticing Joe's self-reproach, and trying to dissuade her obvious burden of guilt. The entire team wholeheartedly agreed and tried to comfort Joe, but the trauma and sadness of the moment drew her further and further inside herself, where she would be lost for some time.

"Where are they now?" Jim asked of Kuuku and his men.

"Those still alive have been rounded up and are being guarded by Hayati and his men. I sent a courier to bring the authorities to take charge of them."

"And Kuuku?" Grace asked, with a strange expectation of dread and relief.

"Gone," Dr. Clark said with some passion. "With this type of scuffle you take out the leader first; that helps to confuse and minimize the fighting courage of the others. They were no match for our modern weaponry."

Search parties were dispatched to find and recover Alan and Yaya's bodies and bring them back to the camp, until appropriate arrangements could be made. Few words were spoken on the way; just a reflective silence, each grieving the loss of his friend in his own way. Joe continued to blame herself for the tragic events of the day, though it was clear to everyone else that the unforeseen circumstances leading up to their heartrending losses were beyond her control.

As soon as they reached Dr. Clark's compound, Dr. Clark instructed Hayati to increase perimeter security, in case any other predatory tribe had unknowingly moved into the area. Grace called Frank to get an update on Piper, and to let everyone back home know the sad news of Alan's death. Then, alone in her room, she took the small USB drive pendent that held her and Frank's vital research from around her neck and reverently held it in her hand. She looked down at it as a flood of tears fell unmercifully from her eyes. *At what cost*, she repeated over and over in her mind, staring at the pendent. *Was it worth it?* Her thoughts drifted. *What just happened? It wasn't supposed to be this way!* Then she remembered his words the day they left: *'I will, Gloria, on my life I will.'* She then hauntingly remembered the scolding she gave Alan and her father for their silly, audacious entrance before leaving, making her already deep regret for insisting on this ill-fated venture even greater. *If only* . . . but it was too late for `what ifs'. Alan was gone, and there was no bringing him back.

Meanwhile Joe was inconsolable. Everyone tired to convince her that the day's disasters were not her fault, but like a wounded animal, she isolated herself from the others, trying to find some means of escape from her troubled, self-reproaching thoughts. None could be found.

Before turning in for the night, Jim found Dr. Clark in the main hall and asked, "Do you think there are any more hostile tribes in this area?"

"I don't think so, but I've doubled the guard just in case."

"Thanks—that will help us all rest easier."

"Think nothing of it."

After saying goodnight to Dr. Clark and those of his staff who were with him, Jim made his way to his daughter's room to see how she was coping with Alan's death.

"You've had a tough go of it, Grace," Jim said, as he shared in his daughter's grief, sitting next to her on the canvas bed under the mosquito netting.

"I'm so torn, Dad," she volunteered vulnerably, with swollen eyes and tears still streaming down her face. "We came to save Piper, but look at the cost!"

"Alan would have gladly sacrificed himself again and again for his Gracie and little Piper. Just keep that in mind, and it will ease the pain in your heart a little; I know it has for me. He was a great friend and a generous, godly man."

"Oh, Dad! He was, and I'll always, always remember."

It was finally Jim's turn to shed his manly pride and veiled outward appearance, breaking down convulsively into his daughter's arms. "He saved my precious daughter! Who could be a better friend?"

The following day Grace woke with a greater sense of purpose, knowing that any further delay would not only impede Piper's chances of survival, but also cause Alan's heroic sacrifice to have been in vain. This mission's success was now more critical than ever; the stakes were doubled. So with a renewed determination in her heart, Grace committed more than ever, if that were even possible, to aggressively pursue and secure Piper's future.

CHAPTER 11

Frank Tells Piper a Story

THE NEWS OF ALAN's passing was hard for those back home. Gloria was particularly affected because of all the years she spent working with Alan on Capitol Hill, testifying and lobbying Congress on behalf of the silent voices of the pre-born. Alan was affectionately known as Uncle Al to Frank and Piper, but it was Piper who was most affected by his death.

Every time Alan would return home from one of his exciting over-seas adventures, he would bring back a few mementos for Piper and tell grand tales of his far-off exploits. Piper's room was filled with these strange and mysterious artifacts: knives and tunics, bows and arrows, headdresses from a variety of different cultures, vases and bowls, toys of all kinds and a host of other rare and not so rare trinkets. Each treasure had a history and reminded Piper of Alan; but most of all, she remembered his many stories about Jesus, and how He loves us so much.

"How are you doing, Piper?" Gloria asked, entering Piper's room and disturbing her melancholy thoughts and memories of days gone by with Alan.

"Sad, Gamma."

"I know, sweetheart; we are all very sad right now. It's hard to believe, isn't it? It's even more difficult with everyone so far away."

"I . . . I miss Mama . . . and p . . . poor Al . . ."

"Yes, we miss them too—very much."

Gloria and Frank decided to inform Piper about Alan sooner rather than later, and broke the news to her as gently as possible. Frank thought a story might help Piper cope with Alan's loss, while Gloria's mind went immediately to a letter Paul had written to his wife Elle years earlier, and how the song Paul shared in it comforted her when she was going through her own grief. So, while Gloria went in search of a copy of that letter, Frank was thinking of how to honor Alan and give meaning to this seemingly meaningless loss. He wanted Piper to understand that even though these bad things happen, God is still good—and only good. But was Frank convinced of it himself? For some reason, in spite of Piper's long-term illness, he never doubted it until now.

How can God be a 'good' God in the midst of all this pain, suffering and death? Frank questioned in his mind. He then quickly realized that it would be difficult to confidently reassure Piper of this truth if he could not fully grasp it himself. So Frank went to work setting out to put feet to his faith and to find clarity for what now seemed to be a very contradictory theology.

First he looked up verses that addressed God's claim to be good. This seemed like the practical place to start and sure enough—a couple jumped out at him right away . . .

Oh, give thanks to the Lord, for He is good! His mercy endures forever. (1 Chronicles 16:34)

And . . .

No one is good but One, that is, God. (Mark 10:18)

This confirms the Bible's claims that He is good, Frank thought; *now to the harder question . . .*

Frank started by researching other religions and how they tried to explain evil and suffering in the world, but without satisfaction. Most either attributed evil to their gods, or taught that good and evil were a natural balancing of life, belying their gods' claim of goodness. Others only offered concepts of meditations and teachings to avoid, or at least reduce, the effects of evil in their lives.

Finding no credible explanation in any other religion of how God can be good with the backdrop of cruelty and suffering plaguing our world, Frank returned to his Christian faith to solve the riddle. The question was where to begin.

Reflecting on his studies of other religions, he noticed a disconnect between their gods and the people worshipping them, with only a human prophet or writing to explain who that god was. There was no direct contact or intimacy that he could observe with any of these other gods, as if all of mankind were just fish in a fishbowl, to be observed from a distance; impersonal, detached . . . loveless.

But that isn't who my God is; I feel Him near, Frank reflected. *I have His Word; and then there is Jesus, not a prophet, but God Himself, and the Holy Spirit!* Frank knew that Jesus's claim to be God was true, but for the sake of clarity and thoroughness, he wanted to verify this claim with specific scriptures . . .

Just as you saw that a Stone was broken off from the Mountain without hands, and that it crushed the iron, the bronze, the clay, the silver, and the gold, the great God has made known to the king what will take place in the future; so the dream is certain, and its interpretation is trustworthy. (Daniel 2:45)

And . . .

The Father and I are one. (John 10:30)

And . . .

This was why the Jews were seeking all the more to kill Him, because not only was He breaking the Sabbath, but He was even calling God His Father, making Himself equal with God. (John 5:18)

Frank had now established God's claim of being good, and Jesus's claim that He was in fact God; now it was time to try to reconcile these facts with the opposing reality of being surrounded in this life by pain, cruelty and death.

In this life? Frank thought. *This is not the only life we are promised.* He continued thinking reflectively and again returned to Scripture to verify this truth . . .

Brothers and Sisters, we do not want you to be uninformed about those who sleep in death, so you do not grieve like the rest of mankind, who have no hope. (1 Thessalonians 4:13)

And . . .

And God shall wipe away all tears from their eyes; and there shall be no more death, neither sorrow, nor crying, neither shall there be any more pain: for the former things have passed away. (Revelation 21:4)

It was true that these and other scriptures gave hope for a life of paradise beyond this messed up world, but that still didn't answer the question he had of this life; the here and now.

Maybe it will become clearer if I start at the beginning, he reasoned; so back to the scriptures he went . . .

God saw all that He had made, and behold, it was very good. And there was evening and there was morning, the sixth day. (Genesis 1:31)

So, at one time there was only good on the earth. What happened?

(God commanded), but from the Tree of the Knowledge of Good and Evil you shall not eat, for the day that you eat from it, you will surely die. (Genesis 2:17)

. . . She took from (the Tree of the Knowledge of Good and Evil) its fruit and ate; she gave also to her husband with her, and he ate. (Genesis 3:6)

So, this was the answer then, this is where death and all the evil in the world were birthed; it was our rebellion and disobedience to the Word of God.

Frank went on to quantify this truth in his mind, that it wasn't the 'lack' of God's goodness that had caused suffering and death, but the `rejection' of God's goodness that caused us to suffer these results.

This is where Frank started to put all the pieces together and develop a story that would help Piper cope with Alan's passing. He wanted to convey that although bad things happened, God does not cause them, and that through Jesus we can be transformed into perfect holiness, health and peace; not only in the here and now, but where Alan was, forever in Heaven.

While Frank was busy writing Piper's story, Grandma Gloria found the portion of Paul's letter she was looking for and would not only share it with Piper, but also send it to Dr. Clark with a note of encouragement to share with those mourning the deaths of Alan and Yaya.

Eventually Frank's story was complete, and Piper was ecstatic, catching wind of it the day before.

"Is it rea . . . dy?" Piper asked with anticipation, as Gloria and Frank walked into her room, with Frank holding some folded papers.

"It is," Frank answered with a smile, enjoying his daughter's eagerness. "It's right here in my hand."

After removing Piper's oxygen tent and getting comfortable, with eager ears, Frank began . . .

"Once upon a time, there was a father with two sons; and although he loved both of his sons with a great love, he couldn't help but be more pleased with one son over the other. You see, his 'Wise' son followed all his rules, realizing his father's rules were meant for good, to protect him and keep him safe, while the 'Foolish' son thought his father's rules were just to spoil his fun. The Foolish son was always breaking an arm or some other bone, getting sick eating poison berries, and even pulling pranks on his Wise brother, causing him to get hurt at times as well, and getting him in trouble with his father. But the Wise son always forgave his Foolish brother.

"Well one day the the Foolish son was playing at the creek near their home, where his father had given him strict orders not to play near the high waterfall, where the water ran swift."

"Foolish b . . . boy d . . . didn't listen . . . did he?"

"No, Piper, he didn't listen," Frank answered, happy to see Piper was getting into the story. "And the Foolish son, curious to look over the edge of the falls to find out what he could see, slipped and fell into the fast-raging water at the edge of the falls, with an array of deadly, jagged rocks perilously scattered far below him. Just in time, however, he grabbed a branch, which kept him from going completely over the edge. But he still wasn't safe. The branch would only hold him for so long before it snapped, sending him to his doom."

Anxiously anticipating what would happen next, Piper gave a gasp, as she envisioned the Foolish son clinging for his life far above the jagged rocks. Frank continued.

"Quickly, the Wise son ran to his brother's rescue, grabbing another branch to pull his Foolish brother to safety. Then to their horror, after the Foolish brother was safe, they heard a cracking sound, as the Wise brother's branch broke, sending him crashing to the rocks below.

"The Foolish son couldn't believe what just happened, as tears fell from his eyes for the first time in his life. Even though he knew he would incur the wrath of his father, he ran as fast as he could to explain what had happened, and, thinking there still may be hope for his brother, get help. But as he saw his weeping father lovingly bending over his Wise son and lifting his lifeless body into his arms, he knew all hope was gone.

"Well, that's enough for today," Frank said, starting to stand up. "We can finish the rest of the story tomorrow."

Piper protested, as her bed shook violently at Frank's jest; the look on Gloria's face clearly showed she was not happy with her son-in-law's little tease either.

"Okay, okay," Frank quickly relented, sitting back down again to finish the story. "I was just kidding."

"Frank," was all Gloria could say, her eyes saying the rest: *boys will be boys!*

"Now the father was very sad and very angry at the Foolish son for causing his Wise son's death," Frank continued, "but to the Foolish son's amazement, his father didn't scold him; instead, he let the Foolish son do anything he wanted; no rules, no punishments, and for a while, he ran wild with this new freedom. After a time, however, something started to happen in his mind. Day after day, while enjoying his rebellious freedom, he noticed the sadness in his father's eyes and started to feel loneliness for his brother. Soon he found himself staying home more to be by his father's side, and to comfort him in his grief. He started to feel his own grief for his brother, and came to fully admit that his own rebellious actions led to his brother's death. He became sad like his father, and by his own choice, started to obey all of his father's rules without even being reminded."

"One day the Foolish son, who was now his father's Wise son, went to his father saying, 'I have sinned against you, and because of that sin, your Wise son, my brother, is dead.'

"The father smiled for the first time since his Wise son's death, and answered, 'My Wise son, we are both now heartbroken over this emptiness in our hearts, but my son, your brother did not die in vain, for it was through his death, that you were transformed from death to life; from being a Foolish son, to the Wise son you are now.' He paused for a moment and then added, "When one dies to save another, it is never a wasted life; it is a good life. Alan gave his life to save your mother's life; that is one of the most noble and honorable ways one could spend a life."

There was only silence, and the clamor of Piper's rhythmic medical machines, as Frank pulled out his Bible. "It says in John 15:13, 'Greater love has no man than this that he lay down his life for his friends.'"

CHAPTER 12

The Cure

"YOU KNOW, GRACE, I wasn't sure I would be able to help you when you first contacted me," Dr. Clark confessed, as they began to upload and organize Grace's files from her USB drive into his computer. "I've spent a year out here in this desolate jungle, and my work is very important to me."

"I know, Doctor, and I'm so sorry to inconvenience you this way, but . . ."

"No, no, don't say another word. Grace; you've paid a high price to get here; besides, the most difficult part of my research is complete, and Tahu is more than capable of taking over the final phases of the work. Everything will be okay—you'll see. By the way, where's Joe? I have something from your mother I want to share with all of you, but especially her."

"My mother?"

"Yes, and I think it will do us all some good."

Dr. Clark found Joe a very reluctant participant, but after much coaxing, gathered her and the research team into the meeting tent, along with Tahu, Hayati and a few other locals that had known Yaya. Joe sat behind everyone, wishing she was anywhere other than in a room full of people she had failed; sensing scorn and contempt from them, a feeling with no basis in truth. Dejected, she stared at the floor, not wanting to make eye contact with anyone. And, although she appeared to be disinterested in what Dr. Clark had to say, nothing could have been further from the truth; she was listening intently to every word, especially when he mentioned that Gloria's message was sent especially for her. She was no longer a 'reluctant' participant, but eager to hear what Grace's mother could possibly say that would encourage her broken heart.

"This morning Grace's mother, Gloria, sent me a message to share with you and Joe in particular," Dr. Clark began. "She felt as we mourn Alan and Yaya's deaths, that we take heart in the words of Alan's one-time best friend, Paul; from a portion of a letter he wrote to his wife Elle, just before he died."

Dr. Clark produced a paper from his pocket, carefully unfolding it and straightening out its seams on his leg. "As I read these words," he continued, "they will have greater meaning and impact on your souls if you hear them as though Alan's heart itself is reaching out to you, to comfort you . . ."

Already in an acutely emotional state, Joe burst into uncontrollable sobs, as Grace, sitting next to her, slipped a loving arm around her. Dr. Clark waited until the storm passed to begin.

"Gloria said that this portion of Paul's letter, the part Elle shared with Alan, originally to mock his friend, eventually meant so much to Alan that he wanted it read at his own funeral someday. Sadly, that day is here."

Alan was greatly respected by all who knew him. With her budding love that had just begun to bloom, Joe in particular would have been overwhelmed enough, but the guilt and shame she carried in her heart due to her conviction that Alan's death was caused by some lack of judgment on her part, made her burden worse. She was tempted to pull away from what she saw as Grace's unwarranted pity; however, she continued to accept Grace's comforting and loving embrace, as Dr. Clark shared Alan's sentiments.

A Daugther's Lament

'Excerpt from Paul's Letter to his wife Elle'

Lyrics to "Don't Weep For Me"

Sooner or later it's time for us to go.
But don't weep for me, for I know where I'm to go.
For you see I've put my trust
In the Creator's hands above,
So when I go, I go in peace
To the Savior that I love.

So don't weep for me. Don't weep for me.
Cry for all those without hope,
Who stumble deep into the night,
Who haven't known the love of God,
Or the mercy of His Light!

But don't weep for me. Don't weep for me.

Jesus is the Way, the Truth the Life,
And if you call on Him you'll never die.
Call on Jesus now today,
While there's time; please don't delay
To make Heaven your home,
And where you'll never be alone!

But don't weep for me. Don't weep for me.
Cry for all those without hope,
Who stumble deep into the night,
Who haven't known the love of God,
Or the mercy of His Light!

Don't weep for me. Don't weep for me.

"In closing, I would like to share the words of Jesus in John 15:13; not at all empty words. For our example they are words of action, through the laying down of His own life on the Cross for each of us; the same action Alan demonstrated by laying down his life for his friends. `Greater love hath no man than this — that he lay down his life for a friend.' Alan did just that, and would want us to look forward, `forgetting the past, and looking forward to the prize that awaits us in Jesus Christ.' Joe," Dr. Clark said, with his full gaze upon her, "No one here blames you for what happened; you are loved and appreciated, and not only that, through your cunning actions and courage, you saved many lives. If he were here, I know beyond a shadow of a doubt, that Alan would be thanking you now, not blaming you."

With these closing words, Joe threw herself on Grace and wept bitterly; but this time they were cleansing tears, as the unwarranted guilt and self-pity that had consumed her began to melt away.

"What have you been working on, if you don't mind me asking?" Grace asked Dr. Clark the following day as they started organizing her research for the task at hand.

"There's a sailor's widow with three young children from my hometown in Peggy's Cove, Nova Scotia. About two years ago, her youngest son started to show symptoms that no local doctor could diagnose. Knowing my field of expertise, she contacted me to look into his condition. I as well was frustrated, and initially at a loss to understand his illness, and that's what led me here; and on the verge of solving the mystery. But enough of my research, you are here to solve your own mystery in saving your daughter, and I am eager to help. Let's get started."

Weeks dragged slowly by, as one failure led to another.

"Don't be discouraged," Dr. Clark urged Grace as she let out a sigh. "These things take time, and we're making good progress."

They were actually making great progress for the comparatively short time they had been working; but Grace only saw each passing day as another that may prove to be the one too late to save

Piper. However, in just six short weeks, both were convinced they had solved the mystery of Piper's condition, and with special FDA approval to bypass the regular drug approval processes, Grace and her companions were ready to start for home with great expectations for Piper.

Joe had recovered dramatically from her self-imposed guilt, thanks to Gloria's encouragement through Paul's letter and her friend's steadfast support. Along with a few of Dr. Clark's troops for added security; she led the team again with confidence back to Tagati, where goodbyes were heartfelt and tearful.

The rut-infested bumpy road back to the Bondoukou airport, was thankfully free of any troubles worth mentioning. It had seemed like years since they had stepped from the plane into the hot and muggy air just a few months earlier, and were glad to be finally heading home. It was a bittersweet parting to be sure, but the anticipation of Piper's cure softened the emptiness of the journey.

CHAPTER 13

Finally Home

IT WAS A BITTERSWEET reunion as Grace and her father stepped from the plane into the brisk and chilly autumn New England air, a stark contrast from the uncomfortable, muggy air they had just left a few hours earlier. In Alan's honor the Ivory Coast government had graciously provided a privately chartered jet for them, and the airport provided a remote area on the tarmac, so Alan's coffin could be privately offloaded and his friends disembark, without the unwanted stares of curious onlookers.

Tears of joy flowed freely as Gloria and Frank stepped from the portable air stairs, embracing their spouses for the first time in months.

A banging noise interrupted their reunion and arrested their attention. They turned to see Alan's casket being unloaded from the plane's cargo hold; new tears now found their way into their eyes.

"Poor Alan," Jim commented about his best friend.

"I still can't believe he's gone, Dad," Grace added. "He saved my life out—out there in the . . ." Grace hesitated, overwhelmed by emotion.

"I know . . ."

"Piper will be so excited to see you both!" Gloria interrupted, desiring to distract their attention away from the somber activity behind them, and toward the anticipation of the joyous homecoming before them.

"Yes, we can't wait," Grace and her father responded together, but with muted excitement as they turned their gaze from the rear of the plane.

"How is our precious little Angel doing?" Jim asked Frank, as they were being escorted from the quiet solitude of the tarmac into the clamor and echoes of the busy gate terminals and corridors inside.

"She's hanging in there," Frank answered, hesitating a little before answering. "But I'm— I'm sure glad you're back; Piper too."

There was inexpressible joy in the Connors' house that afternoon, mingled with the sad loneliness and absence of Piper's 'Uncle Al.' The next day Frank and Grace went to work right away, preparing the serum for Piper that had come at such a high cost. The interruption of Alan's funeral was the only distraction they would allow, wanting to organize and schedule the dosing protocol as quickly as possible, slowly introducing Piper's immune system to the new medication.

"I'm scared," Grace said, looking up at Frank before administering the first dose. "What if it doesn't work? What if . . ."

"Shhh," Frank answered softly, drawing her close. "We'll save the 'what ifs' for another time. For now, we will trust . . ."

"But her life . . . her life is in my hands."

"God's hands," Frank reminded her. "All we are called to do is to do the best we can in faith, leaving the rest to God; and that is what we've done—our best. Now we must step out in faith."

"Frank," Grace looked up trembling, putting her hand in his. "Let's pray . . ."

The uncertain days that followed were wearing on everyone's nerves. In Piper's already- lethargic physical condition, it was hard to determine the effect of the serum one way or the other. They knew a positive reaction would be hard to recognize in the early stages of the process, so all they could do was hope and wait.

Grace jumped nervously every time Piper would moan or cough, or if there was even a slight fluctuation of the monotonous beeping tones of the monitors surrounding her bed. Dr. Clark was daily consulted on her progress or lack thereof, and for many frustrating weeks there seemed to be no significant change in Piper's condition, good or bad. They were all puzzled at this, but at the same time thankful no negative side effects had developed.

"Be patient," Dr. Clark encouraged, as the days and weeks crawled by slowly. "Piper has been in this condition a long time, and it only makes sense that it will take time for her body to respond."

Daily increasing the dosage as prescribed by Dr. Clark, Grace prayed over each one as it was administered.

"How do you feel today, my little Angel?" Grace would ask each morning.

"The same," Piper would respond with an enduring smile and contagious; hopeful optimism. "I know J . . . Jesus will heal m . . . me."

Day after day, Piper gave the same answer, as Grace and the others waited patiently for even a minor hint of a positive change in her condition.

"She isn't getting worse," Jim said to Grace consolingly one morning, in his own encouraging, ever-optimistic way.

"That is true," Grace responded, trying to share her father's optimism, but hardly equal to the task.

More days went by with little change, until Dr. Clark suggested a small alteration in the serum's chemical makeup and dosage protocol. These minor changes seemed to make all the difference in the world as Piper's condition started to improve, though very slightly at first, then significantly. Soon Piper was able to sit up in bed on her own, roll from side to side, and her speech, well . . .

"Good morning, Mama," Piper chirped one morning, as clear as could be.

"Good morning to you, my little princess," Grace answered, with tears of joy streaming down her cheeks.

"If only Uncle Al could see me now!" Piper said, showing off her newly acquired flexibility and strength. "He would be so happy!"

"He would for sure, my little Angel."

Soon the plastic bubble that had been Piper's claustrophobic bed covering for too many years was removed, along with all the monitors and equipment surrounding her bed; they were simply no longer needed. Within a few days Piper was able to move from her bed to a nearby couch, where she would read and draw on her I-pad for hours at a time. Every advancement and milestone was faithfully recorded in her journal and celebrated as though it was her first, until the big day finally arrived: her first steps.

Piper's inability to move on her own for years caused acute atrophy in the muscles throughout her body, even though Trisha, a physical therapist hired when Piper's symptoms first developed, had been working with her all along. Now, all her hard work was finally paying off, as Piper's mobility quickly improved.

"Are you sure it's okay? Do you think she's ready?" A concerned Grace asked while looking at Trisha hesitantly.

"Ask her," she responded with a wink and a nod in Piper's direction.

"I'm more than ready, Mama!" Piper responded, with a big, confident smile of anticipation.

"Okay, but this momentous occasion deserves an audience," Grace said, calling for the rest of the family to witness this hugely significant milestone in Piper's life.

"You can do it!" Grandma Gloria called out. Then, Grace and Frank chimed in, cheering her on, as Piper was lifted from her bed to the floor.

"You've got this! You can do it!" A chorus of heartfelt, encouraging voices continued to ring in her ears, as Piper tried with all her might to take that first step.

"I . . . I can't do it," Piper admitted as she tried repeatedly to drag her foot forward.

Although Piper was unable to put her full weight on her legs or balance on her own in this first attempt, you might have thought she had just completed a triathlon, for all the celebration that followed. It wasn't long, however, and Piper did take her first step, eventually walking, then running, and then skipping her way through the house as though she had been walking and running for years. It was evident that Piper had made a full recovery, thanks to the plethora of prayers, the skill of Dr. Clark, the courage and steadfastness of her mother, and a host of others who had sacrificed so much to achieve this positive outcome—especially Uncle Al.

"I wish Uncle Al could see me now!" Piper exclaimed to her mom exuberantly one day, as she ran and danced through the kitchen into the living room.

"I'm sure he can," Grace answered, overwhelmed with gratitude.

Life couldn't have been better for the Connors. Besides Piper's full recovery, they had their living room back; they were both employed again, had paid off their debts, and looked forward to a carefree life; at least more carefree than it had been since the onset of Piper's illness. Piper was also excited, and she greatly anticipated a little brother or sister playmate, as Grace and Frank were expecting their second child.

Dr. Clark, Joe and Alan were often on their minds as the months and years elapsed. Grateful to each for their unique sacrifice to bring this miracle healing to Piper, the Connors often spoke of the three and reminisced. From time to time Dr. Clark and Joe would even fly in from Nova Scotia and the Ivory Coast to visit their little Angel.

Life had finally settled into a normal routine for the Connors, with only a vague memory of those sad days of long ago. There were church meetings, school, holidays and birthdays, which were especially celebrated. And then there were Piper's little sisters, Faith and Joy; the twins. They were as healthy as could be—and inseparable. Life was good . . .

. . . or was it?

CHAPTER 14

Rude Awakening

"GRACE! GRACE, WAKE UP!" a familiar voice yelled intensely, as a wild banging of the door vibrated through the entire room as it swung open.

It was three o'clock in the morning, and though the intense, animated call dazed Grace for a moment, her sleeping stupor wouldn't allow her to stir. The day before had been an extraordinarily exhausting one, and the adrenalin required to survive it made her so over-tired; she couldn't fall asleep without a sleeping aid until after midnight.

"Grace!" the voice rang out again pleadingly. "I woke Frank an hour ago, because I didn't know what to do, but something's very wrong! We need your help immediately!"

Grace tried to open her eyes to see what the ruckus was about, but the intense, bright light that the eerie, shadowy figure had flipped on when entering the room sent a painful glare into her eyes, making it even harder to focus.

"What is it?" Grace finally uttered with a slur, shading her tired eyes from the piercing light, and then asked in her delirium, "Who are you?"

"Grace!" The eerily familiar phantom voice pleaded again, "Piper is having bad convulsions, and nothing we've done is helping!"

"Piper? Convulsions?" Startled and confused, Grace sat up, still blinded by the glare. *She hasn't had seizures in years, ever since,*

since . . . Since when? And what is so familiar about this voice? Grace reflected for a moment, her mind spinning in confusion. It had been so long since Piper had had any symptoms or been sick; she couldn't quantify what this apparition was trying so desperately to communicate. *Was she dreaming, or just waking up from one?* An incoherent fog surrounded her whirling thoughts.

"Where's Grace?" Another familiar voice yelled in a panic through the doorway. This voice she recognized as her husband's. "Alan! Why isn't she up yet? Piper needs her now!"

Alan? Alan? Grace questioned in her mind, *Alan died years ago. Who's this Alan?* Her mind, still in a half-awakened dazed bewilderment, couldn't comprehend Frank's bizarre command, until she reluctantly began to recognize the stranger's voice and put two-and-two together. *That voice, it 'is' Alan's voice, my Alan. But how?* Slowly, the sleepy fog in her eyes cleared to reveal the familiar outline of Alan's face. She started to comprehend this new reality into which she had just awakened. *I'm not dreaming! This is real! Alan is real! But . . . if, if this is real! Then, Africa, Dr. Clark, the cure! It all never happened? No Dr. Clark! No cure! That means . . . Piper is still . . . ; it was all for nothing!* This last thought jolted away what remained of her sleepy haze. She jumped out of bed and rushed toward Piper's room in a panic.

This is impossible! She groaned in despair as she looked in. Just a moment ago my baby was dancing through the house!

Alan's shadowy figure was now as clear as day. There was no doubt; she had passed from a bittersweet dream life to a stark, cold reality. Alan was alive, but Piper, Piper was still fighting for her life!

Grace gasped as she stumbled over the threshold, staggering under the revelation of what her eyes refused to believe. There was that same horrid, plastic oxygen tent covering her hospital bed, and the all-too familiar monitors with their monotonous rhythms. She reached for the doorframe to steady herself, as her legs began to buckle under her. *A dream? A dream like my mom's?* She groaned inaudibly.

"Grace, what is it?"

At that moment her husband's voice distracted her overwhelmed mind from the what if, to the what is, as a violent shaking of the plastic cover and a cry of pain solidified the overwhelming truth that this was indeed her new undeniable reality. She dropped her face into her hands in despair, tears coursing down her cheeks. Her emotions fluctuated from one extreme to another; and though paralyzed with fear and confusion, she instinctively knew what was required at the moment: Piper needed her!

Having helped Piper through many of these episodes in the past, Grace worked skillfully but mechanically, restoring the tranquil peace to both Piper and the night. Another race was on to save Piper's life, but this time, it wasn't a dream.

"Grace, are you alright? Frank asked, concerned and knowing something was terribly wrong, yet thankful she had pulled herself together and was coherent enough to help Piper through this latest episode.

"Who did you think I was?" Alan asked, curious at Grace's earlier perplexed and fearful look at seeing his shadowy figure.

But instead of answering, Grace buckled under the weight of all her recent physical and mental strain, fainting and collapsing to the floor.

It was late the next day before Grace awoke from her death-like dreamless sleep, unconsciously moaning and calling out for Faith and Joy.

Being a little more clear-minded after her long rest, Grace shared her dream in as much detail as she could later that evening, with her parents, Frank and Alan.

"Of course, Alan, I'm so glad you're still alive, but to see Piper like that again, when in my dream she was so full of life, running and dancing, well my heart just broke!"

"I can't imagine the shock it must have been, waking up to see a sick and suffering Piper again," Alan said sympathetically. Grace looked up through her tears; happy he was with them, instead of in a casket being unloaded off a tarmac. "But, I am thankful," Alan added with his usual wit, "that I don't have a spear protruding from my chest right now."

Everyone laughed at Alan's attempt at humor. Even Grace was able to crack a smile for the first time since awaking from her dream. But inside Grace silently lamented over Piper's seemingly hopeless future and continued failing health.

"Before I forget, I'm going to write down what Dr. Clark and I had discovered in my dream," Grace confided to Frank that evening. "Even though it was only a dream, some of the ideas we came up with have merit and actually make sense. I think my 'dream notes' may be helpful as we move forward.

"You think so?" Frank responded skeptically.

"I know it's a long shot, but some of the concepts Dr. Clark and I discovered in Africa, well, I mean in my dream, may be worth pursuing."

"You know that Dr. Clark isn't real," Frank said, lowering his brows and narrowing his eyes, putting on a suspicious look, playfully conveying doubt as to her sanity.

"Oh, Frank," Grace replied incredulously, crossing her eyes and returning her own playful animated look of a crazed zombie.

"Well, we might as well give this non-existent doctor's ideas a try," Frank retorted, continuing his bantering. "We've hit a road-block, so we might as well give your 'dream doctor' a try."

In the meantime Alan couldn't quite get this daring and courageous Joe person that Grace had related in her dream out of his mind. His adventurous life had been getting a little lonely of late, and this Joe character started his mind thinking that maybe it was time to move on with his life and settle down again. For the fun of it he went on a few dating sites, setting the filter to only bring up women with names of Joe or Josephine. *This is so juvenile,* he thought to himself after a few awkward chats, and he quickly gave up that direction of meeting his special future someone. *God will provide,* he mused, *though I doubt if He will bring me someone named Joe,* he finally concluded with a hearty laugh.

Frank helped Grace compile all the information that she could glean from her dream, amazed at how technically deep and detailed the information ended up being. They both saw a clear new avenue forward, revitalizing a hope, that until Grace's dream, had faded into despair and hopelessness. Research began again in earnest, as day after day new discoveries led them into new possibilities.

One night, as Grace and Frank were intensely pursuing this new avenue of research, Frank's expression suddenly changed into one of contorted confusion and astonishment, as he sat motionless, staring at his computer screen.

"Grace?" He finally blurted out impulsively. "What was the name of your dream doctor?"

"Dr. Clark. Why do you ask?"

"No, I mean his full name?" Frank pressed impatiently, ignoring her question.

Upon hearing this unexpected request, Grace immediately turned to see a bizarre look on her husband's face.

She hesitated for a moment before answering, trying to comprehend the meaning of the look on her husband's face. "It was Dr. William C. Clark. But what's wrong? You look like you've seen a ghost!"

"I might have," Frank said, pointing to his laptop and turning it a little, so Grace could more easily see what he had discovered.

CHAPTER 15

Deja-vu

GRACE MOVED CLOSER TO see where Frank was pointing. *Dr. William C. Clark will be coming out of retirement to participate in this year's Global Health Summit, a rare privilege for those who know him and his work . . .*

"Wow," Grace exclaimed, and laughed in amazement at the almost impossible coincidence that she was seeing right before her eyes. "That's interesting, Frank, but darling, it's just a coincidence . . . isn't it?" Grace questioned, still curious and perplexed by the contorted ghostly pallor on her husband's face.

"Grace, look again," Frank replied, drawing her attention back to the screen as he scrolled down the page to reveal more of the text . . .

. . . His many successes and breakthroughs in the study and cure of rare childhood diseases have impressed the medical community for decades, and he will be at the GHS next month . . .

Grace was speechless. She didn't have to read any farther to understand Frank's stupefaction. Disbelief enveloped her own mind now, as her face began to quickly emulate that of her husband's. "How can this be?" she asked almost inaudibly, as their eyes met. "Frank, can this even be possible? Am I having another dream?"

"If you are, I'm right in there with you." He chuckled, wondering the same thing to himself.

But it was possible, and the only thing different between Grace's dream doctor and this new real-life one, were their ages.

Grace's jungle doctor was young, while this other Dr. Clark, according to the article, had already been in retirement for some time.

"Frank, do you think we should . . ."

"Yes, I do. We'll look him up first thing tomorrow . . ."

However, trying to get in contact with a well-known retired doctor who cherishes his privacy and seclusion, proved to be harder than either Grace or Frank could have imagined. To make things worse, the article that Frank had stumbled upon was over a year old. Every possible lead had been followed to find this 'real' Dr. Clark, without success. Even contacting the site that had originally posted the article was a dead end, as they had no personal information to share in regards to Dr. Clark. They also discovered that the original author of the article had died a year earlier in a motorcycle accident, leading to yet another dead end.

Then they discovered the medical institute in New York, where he had conducted his research for the last twenty years, only to be informed that it was against hospital policy to share personal information with non-family members.

This went on for days, following one clue after another, with one disappointment after another. Finally, they turned to a private investigation agency for help.

We'll probably find him retired deep in the jungles of some remote region in Africa, Grace mused in frustration, wondering if she would have to go through another jungle adventure to find another illusive Dr, Clark. Yet she knew in the dark recesses of her unconscious mind that she would do it all over again, and more, for her precious Piper.

Meanwhile, Piper continued to fail, with her seizures becoming more frequent and intense. Frank and Grace were desperate, exhausted and discouraged.

"I know God can heal in many different ways," Grace said to her husband one day after helping Piper through another painful convulsive fit, and experiencing another disappointing day of failing to locate Dr. Clark. "He heals through the immune system, T-cells, diet, medication and even the supernatural. Are we missing something?"

Frank reflected a moment. "Well, Piper's natural immune system is incapable of fighting off whatever attacks her, her diet is pure, and we haven't discovered a medical cure yet. Failing that, we've been praying earnestly and daily for a supernatural intervention. So I don't think we have."

All Grace could do in response to that seemingly thorough and well thought-out answer was merely to heave a frustrated sigh of sad agreement.

But, had they been missing something?

"Alan says he has a surprise for us and is stopping over later tonight," Frank said, turning to Grace and putting down his phone.

"A surprise, huh?" Grace answered whimsically, with a suppressed chuckle. "Blonde or brunette?"

"Ha, ha, you're funny."

"Well, he did say he was 'back in the hunt', so to speak."

"That's true I guess; maybe you are right," Frank conceded. "Anyway, we'll find out later whether your woman's intuition has failed you or not."

"Not likely on this no-brainer." Grace smiled confidently.

Just then Piper needed their attention, so the speculation on Alan's mysterious news would have to wait.

While Grace and Frank were meeting Piper's immediate needs, Grace's parents, Gloria and Jim, were kneeling by a gravestone at the Crestview Cemetery.

"Our Jeni would have been twenty-seven years old today, if she were still with us," Gloria remarked, in honor of their cherished daughter.

There were many regrets, and they still missed her passionately, though having never seen her. Guilt was no longer an issue; Gloria had found forgiveness in Jesus long before Grace was even born, twenty-six years earlier. It was the 'what ifs' that haunted and preoccupied her mind at times, causing an empty loneliness for her little Jeni. It was after Grace was born that this loneliness became more acute and real to her. It was as though Gloria lived Jeni's life through Grace's. They would have been about the same age, learning and growing at about the same pace; and although sisters are generally quite different from one other, she could imagine, at least in a vague way, what life with Jeni might have been like.

"Do you mind if we stay a little longer, Jim?"

"Take all the time you need."

A flash of lightning and a peal of thunder interrupted Gloria and Jim's visit with their little girl, while several miles away a cloudburst of rain pummeled Alan's car as he drove into the Connors' driveway.

"We'll know soon enough whether your premonition is right or not," Frank said, turning to Grace after hearing Alan's car door slam and footsteps splashing up to the front door, "Alan's here."

Alan was alone as Grace and Frank ushered him quickly in out of the rain, raising some doubt that his visit was romantic in nature.

"Well, that rainstorm hit suddenly, didn't it," Alan commented as he took off his wet shoes, setting them down neatly in the foyer. Frank gave Grace a playful criticizing smirk that she knew instinctively was his opinion of her woman's intuition, or lack thereof. She returned an indifferent shrug, acknowledging her defeat with an acquiescent playful squint of the eyes.

"I have some great news that I wanted to confirm before I got your hopes up," Alan began as soon as they were settled in the living room.

The earnest intensity in his voice evidenced an excitement that couldn't be misunderstood; they knew a great revelation was about to be shared. The thunder storm continued to rage outside, but the anticipation of Alan's news, whatever it was, shut the clamor of that outer world from their minds.

"That's why I couldn't tell you over the phone."

"Is it about Piper?" Grace asked with anticipation.

"Yes!" Alan burst out, "We found him! "

"Found who . . . ?" Frank asked, "You mean . . ."

"Yes. I found Dr. Clark, or I should say Smith did."

"Smith?" Grace asked curiously in her excitement.

"Yes, that's what we call him anyway; Tom Smith, a senate buddy of mine on the Primary Health and Retirement Security

Committee. I still keep in touch with him sometimes and act as a consultant. He has agreed to meet with you!"

"Smith or Dr. Clark?" Frank asked, not exactly sure to whom Alan was referring

"Dr. Clark, of course!" Alan said with a laugh, realizing his lack of clarity. "He lives in Sally's Cove Newfoundland, in Canada. Here's his information."

Alan handed Grace a folded slip of paper.

"Thank you so much, Alan," Grace and Frank expressed exuberantly.

"We'll tell Piper the good news and call him first thing tomorrow," Frank said, reaching out his hand to grasp Alan's in a firm and hardy handshake. Meanwhile, Grace gifted him with a grateful kiss on the cheek. "Thank you again so much!"

CHAPTER 16

Finding the Real
Dr. William C. Clark

THE FOLLOWING DAY THE obviously inept private detective was summarily dismissed, and an early call set in motion a trip out of the country in search of yet another Dr. William C. Clark. Ironically, Grace's meeting would need to be postponed for a week or so, because Dr. Clark was out of the country in Africa on an urgent matter.

They finally received word that he had returned home, but just after Grace had booked an early flight to Canada, Piper had another severe epileptic attack, causing Grace to cancel the flight and delay her departure for yet another day. This added frustration and the increased intensity of Piper's most recent attack, caused Grace to doubt whether meeting with this new doctor, which she considered just another hopeless shot-in-the-dark, was worth leaving Piper for even a day.

"She's stable again. You should go right away," Frank insisted.

"But Frank, what if . . ."

"Grace, every day is a what-if. What if you have an accident on the way to the airport? What if the plane crashes on the way? What if . . ."

"Okay, okay, I get it." Grace surrendered.

"Besides," Frank stressed, "do we really have a choice? This is Piper's last chance. Without Dr. Clark, we . . ."

"I know, Frank. It's so easy to fall into fear and despair, when hope is just on the horizon, only to be dashed over and over again."

Frank drew his wife close, wiping away a tear that had found its way down her cheek. Shattered nerves and repeated disappointment had taken their toll.

"Hope has seen us through this far, and hope will see us through again."

"You remind me of my dad, the eternal optimist," Grace postulated as she snuggled affectionately into her husband's arms.

"You'll see, my little Gracie; everything will be okay. You just wait . . ."

Spring was in the air as Grace stepped out of the plane onto the tarmac. The trees lining the airport drive hovered over them in full bloom, with velvety shades of lavenders and pinks all around her. *This seems more surreal than my dream,* she thought as the cab pulled up to take her to the Clarks'. She was all nerves but didn't know exactly why. Maybe it was because the path to bring her to this point had been so long and the expectations so great? Or, maybe it was Dr. Clark's notoriety and reputation? It might be the fact that she was closer than ever to saving her precious daughter's life? She wasn't sure; all she knew was that her stomach felt like it was twisted into several knots, and she hoped the anxiety she was feeling would not cause her to make a negative first impression on the good doctor.

Distracting herself from these anxious thoughts, she gazed out at the beautiful ocean, with the white cap of its waves spraying and shimmering in the bright sunshine. The deep blue, cloudless sky stretched high above her as she watched the seagulls glide, dive or swoop, doing whatever they did to entertain themselves. Then in amazement, at the end of a long storm break, she saw a magnificent lighthouse, white like marble, tall and majestic with its magnificent glass tower perched high above, the sun's rays glistening through it in all its grandeur.

The oceanfront was a flurry of activity with people walking leisurely up and down its boardwalk, stopping at its many quaint weather-beaten shops, or just sitting on the grass enjoying the picturesque view. Oh, how Grace wished her life could have been so carefree, so normal, but *maybe someday*, she thought. She pictured Frank and Piper walking with her on the wooden planking along the ocean, past the budding trees and copious, colorful flowers. *Someday*, she thought, *maybe someday*.

"We're here, miss," the cabby announced, stirring Grace from her distant dream-world, as he pointed out a charming little stone house, framed beautifully on either side with mature Black Spruce, and a flower garden with a winding cobblestone path leading to the front door.

She paid the cabby and walked nervously up the elegant sidewalk between the immaculate beds of meticulously kept mayflowers, purple violets and numerous other flowers indigenous to that region. Grace was wondering what to say; would he like her, or see her as an intruder disturbing his tranquil, retired life? This was Piper's last chance. *I have to make a good impression*, she thought. Then suddenly, having not even reached ten paces toward the beautifully arched shiny, hunter green door, it flew open.

"We've been expecting you." A slender gray-haired woman greeted Grace with a warm, welcoming gesture, ushering her through the wide open door into her home. "I'm Mrs. Clark; you must be Grace. Please make yourself at home and have some of these refreshments, while I go get William, ah, I mean, Dr. Clark."

It seemed to Grace that Mrs. Clark was more nervous to meet her, than for her to meet Mrs. Clark. She took a gander at what appeared to be the main living room. The sun shone through the leaded windows, flashing a rainbow effect throughout the room against the ornate woodwork and furniture, though old-fashioned, had an aristocratic appeal to them.

"We are so excited to meet you, Grace. May we address you that familiarly, I hope?" Dr. Clark asked, as he entered the room.

"Yes, ah, yes of course," Grace answered, taken aback even more by the intimacy of this honored greeting.

"You wouldn't know this of course; they keep these things fairly close to the vest, if you know what I mean . . ."

"Of course she doesn't know what you mean, William dear," Mrs. Clark interrupted.

"Oh yes, of course she wouldn't, my dear. Let me explain."

Upon witnessing the charming dynamics of this delightful older couple, Grace almost laughed out loud. This was not at all what she had expected and wondered what this mysterious honor was that they seemed to be bestowing upon her.

"Well, like I was saying, you didn't know it at the time; they keep those things rather secret . . ."

"William, will you just get on with it," Mrs. Clark interrupted again, with a nudge.

"Yes dear, I'm getting to it." Dr. Clark said, giving his wife a couple of loving light taps on her hand with a gesture of patience. "You see, Grace, I had the honor of being on the review board that granted you your license to practice medicine; the youngest to ever pass, that I could remember anyway at the time. Well, ever since I have been loosely following your career from a distance."

"Loosely," Mrs. Clark cut in with a laugh. "He's been a fan of yours ever since the night he came home all excited, and told me about this smart young genius of a girl doctor, who was hardly old enough to vote."

Grace blushed and was astonished at this admission, as Dr. Clark continued.

"But until Senator Smith contacted me, I had no Idea that your daughter was so sick."

"William, I said," Mrs. Clark interrupted again, "we must contact this girl at once and see if there's anything we can do to help that poor suffering child of hers. I did indeed; that's what I said!"

"Oh, you are both so wonderful," Grace responded, gratitude emanating through her expressive smile. "Thank you, Mrs. Clark."

"Now, now, no more of that Mrs. Clark stuff, Grace, you call me May, just like everyone else around here does. Isn't that right, William?"

"By all means, dear. Consider our home yours, Grace; and let's get to work right away on seeing what we can do to cure that daughter of yours and get her on the road to recovery!"

"Thank you both," Grace said, again with a look of appreciation that needed no explanation.

"I'll show you to your room so you can get settled; then we'll have a long talk about your daughter and what we can do for her," May said, directing Grace down a short hallway.

"Stay here?" Grace gasped in surprise, not wanting to impose or be a burden to the Clarks. "But, my luggage . . . it's already been, it's not here, it's been, I sent it to the, Inn By The Sea!"

"Oh, nonsense," Dr. Clark protested. "Besides, it will be a lot more efficient if you're right here with us. We'll call Harry, and he will have your luggage brought over in a jiffy."

"William, you call Harry, while I show Grace to her room," May commanded in her own unique, motherly way, while bidding Grace to follow.

How could Grace say no to such a generous and kind offer, as well as the doctor's wise assertion that ideas and thoughts could be more quickly analyzed and reviewed, if they were right there together to quickly evaluate them.

"I don't know what to say, May," Grace floundered, overwhelmed by the Clarks' hospitality as she stepped into the guest room.

"There's nothing to say," May replied, in a tone that if responded to, would have been an insult.

After a quick phone call to Harry, and after devouring a few Purity's Jam-Jams and Crispy Cream Crackers, the Clarks were ready to learn more about Piper, her condition, and the long hard-fought journey that had led Grace eventually to them.

CHAPTER 17

Confessions

"You sit here," May directed, inviting Grace with a gesture to a comfortable high–back, floral-patterned Victorian chair, with a delicately embroidered doily placed neatly over its back, while the Clarks made themselves comfortable on a matching sofa across from her.

"Thank you for sending Piper's charts and her medical history ahead of time," Dr. Clark began. "It has helped me to get a head start on evaluating her condition."

"How is she doing?" May joined in, knowing her husband at times could be all business and his bedside manner at times lacked the empathy and personal touch his patients so often needed.

"Thank you so much for asking," Grace responded appreciatively, as William caught the corrective glimpse from his wife, which communicated a 1000-gig Flash Drive of implication. "She's not doing well at all," Grace answered soberly, but with a gleam of hope in her eyes. "We haven't given up yet."

"Nor should you, Grace, from what I've seen of her case so far," Dr. Clark encouraged.

"It's too late to dive right away into your work," May interrupted, as she noticed the cross-sections of the front windowpanes casting disfigured square shadows on the wall behind Grace. "You and William can get started just as well in the morning; for now, tell us a little bit about yourself."

"Yes, May, I agree; it would be helpful to know a little bit about your background, as well as Piper's." Dr. Clark acquiesced to the obvious direction the evening was going, though he would have preferred getting down to business.

"How old is Piper, and when did you first start noticing something was wrong?" May inquired with anticipation, as only one mother to another could fully appreciate.

Grace went on to explain that the symptoms were hard to notice at first, and that Frank brushed it off as the normal ebb-and-flow of child development, but it soon became apparent that something was seriously wrong. The Clarks occasionally responded with a sympathetic 'poor girl', an 'oh my' or 'you poor dear', as Grace unfolded the suffering and frustrations that both Piper and the rest of the family had endured over the years. And then there was the dream . . .

"I saw 'Dream Notes' in your folder," Dr. Clark inquired, when Grace reached that part of the story. "What are those?"

"Oh yes, the dream," Grace responded reflectively. "I'm not sure just how much of that part of the story will help, but it was your 'dream son', that's what I call him, that helped me discover the antidote that cured Piper; in my dream that is."

"Dream son?" May asked, surprised.

"Oh yes," Grace answered apologetically. "I am getting a little ahead of myself I'm afraid. It was my dream of your namesake that led me to you."

"Namesake?" Dr. Clark inquired.

"Who is this Dream Son of ours?" May asked, confused but with a curiosity that belied a common ordinary interest.

"This dream seems rather interesting," Dr. Clark spoke out, interrupting his wife's desire to learn more about this dream son of hers.

"But why do you call him our son?" May asked, leaning forward with a look of surprise and horror.

"May, what is it . . . ?" Her husband started to inquire, when Grace dropped the bombshell.

"Because he is what led me to you. In my dream his name was Dr. William C. Clark."

May looked away; her body started to heave with every breath. Grace couldn't see with May's back turned, but she knew instinctively that tears were streaming down her face.

"What did I say? What did I do wrong?" Grace gasped, as May excused herself and ran from the room.

"Nothing, Grace. You did nothing wrong," Dr. Clark said, giving her a couple of consoling pats on her shoulder, before excusing himself and getting up to follow his wife from the room.

Back home, they were having their own troubles. With Grace gone, Piper was being more irritable, her convulsions more regular, and even with Gloria's and Alan's full-time help, nerves were stretched to the breaking point. They had all agreed however, not to call Grace, or even hint that Piper's condition had taken a desperate turn for the worse, knowing she would abandon her work with Dr. Clark, and leave for home immediately.

"Don't let on when she calls," Alan told Frank, "If she leaves now, all hope is lost!"

So as the days drearily passed, they kept Piper's desperate and quickly declining condition to themselves.

"I think it's time we check Piper into the hospital; her care is beyond what we can provide any longer," Alan suggested one morning about a week later.

"If only Grace were here," Gloria suggested.

"No," Frank insisted, with Alan's approval. "Grace must not be disturbed at any cost."

Ignorant of the life and death struggle her daughter was facing, Grace sat uncomfortably, guilt-ridden and fearful, as she wondered what she had said that upset Mrs. Clark to such an extent. *There must be some reasonable explanation* she thought, as an embarrassing flush of crimson pulsed uncomfortably through her veins, not knowing why and wishing for an immediate explanation to calm her nerves. She looked at the front door and felt like running away, *but what good would that do?* The seconds turned into minutes, but to Grace they felt like hours before Dr. Clark finally reappeared.

"Now, don't be alarmed," Dr. Clark said, seeing Grace was troubled by May's mysterious sudden outburst and departure. "May is just fine and will explain everything when she feels more herself in a few minutes."

Both sat awkwardly silent for a minute; then, just as Grace started to raise her hand to get Dr. Clark's attention . . .

"Grace dear, you have nothing to apologize for—does she, William?" May questioned, entering the room with the sweetest, sympathetic tone in her voice, still wiping a few stubborn tears from her eyes.

"No dear, she doesn't, not at all," Dr. Clark answered endearingly, with the most empathetic and delicate warmth that Grace had ever heard one spouse use when speaking to another. She even felt a jealous twinge go through her as she smiled within herself.

"Honey dear, do you want to tell Grace about, why, ah, or should I . . . ?"

"I just don't think . . . William—you, I can't . . ."

"All right, dear," William said, yielding to the appeal he saw in his wife's pleading eyes. The lump in May's throat made it impossible for her to say more.

What could it be, Grace wondered, *that made her so upset?*

CHAPTER 18

Dr. William Christopher Clark Jr.

"You see, when we, my precious May and I were in medical school," Dr. Clark began, "all we could think about was ourselves; when we would be graduating and the success of our future careers. We were young and selfish and hadn't learned what was truly important in life."

Dr. Clark moved a little closer to his wife, gently placing his hand on hers, as their eyes met briefly; knowing his selfish immaturity is what ultimately led to the crisis they were now sharing with Grace.

As Dr. Clark looked into May's eyes for that instant, Grace noticed a look of self-reproach and a subtle plea of forgiveness mixed with guilt, especially on May's part. She didn't understand this look at first, but knew instinctively it was a subject of deep regret. She was honored by the openness and vulnerability of this dear couple; to be trusted with what was clearly a long-held, unresolved secret from their past.

"Thank you for allowing us to be so forward with you this way," May said, finally finding the words to speak. "It's been so long since we've talked about William Jr. . . ."

At the mention of what Grace could only assume was their son: William Jr., May again choked on tears that were fighting to escape her eyes, cutting off her ability to speak. Grace wondered who this son could be, and what kind of regretful tragedy could have happened to distress the Clarks so traumatically, May especially.

After a light, comforting squeeze of May's hand, Dr. Clark continued. "We foolishly married when we were still only interns and still years away from any meaningful careers. Not that we regret one day of our marriage though; isn't that right, dear?" May looked up with a warm, affirmative smile in spite of a mist of tears that had finally fought their way out. Dr. Clark drew her close and went on. "Well, May came to class one day with an odd look on her face. Her eyes betrayed a ghostly pallor of panic, yet shone with a glow of excitement; it all contributed toward the strangest smile I had ever seen. She still has the most captivating smile in the world," the doctor interjected. May, blushing and embarrassed, quickly covered that still-captivating smile, which involuntarily beamed from behind her hand at her husband's praise. "Anyway, she just blurted out to me, 'I'm pregnant', as tears of joy fell from her eyes; a joy I crushed with my obvious, cruel disappointed reaction."

This time it was May's turn to lay a comforting hand on his.

"If we could only go back, I . . ."

"William didn't react very well to the news at first, but he was so wonderful later, after the reality of the situation had time to sink in," May interjected, as her husband took this opportunity to compose himself. "But what were we to do? Remember what you said, dear."

"I do; May, I said, you do what you feel is right." Dr. Clark turned to Grace, now his eyes wet with tears of his own. "What you feel is right?" he repeated, "What do feelings have to do with it, when it comes to someone's life!"

"It was the most awful decision of our lives," May interposed, continuing the narrative. "I didn't know it at the time, but William wanted to have our baby in the worst way, even if it did affect our careers. You see back then, it was all about women's rights and it's your body, and all that stuff. So, that's what William did—he honored my choice—by not telling me how much he wanted me to have our baby."

"At the time I didn't want to influence her decision by telling her how I felt."

"And I thought that William's silence meant he didn't want our baby complicating our lives and careers, so . . . so for his sake," May looked longingly and repentantly into her husband's eyes, "I chose to . . . to abort our little baby."

Grace was amazed that May could even get the words out as she was so overcome with regret and sadness. Grace finally understood the connection between May's abortion and the other William; her dream doctor. Grace wasn't a stranger to the deep grief and guilt there can be for a woman after an abortion. She had heard all about her own mother's sorrow and despondency over her little sister Jeni's abortion, her mom's dream about little Jeni, and the dark struggles she went through to come to terms with what she had done; finally finding peace and forgiveness in Jesus.

"Of course I can't relate to what you're going through, "Grace said compassionately, "but, my mom went through exactly the same regrets and guilt as you are feeling now with my little sister Jeni."

"Your mother named her baby; your sister?" May asked, somewhat confused.

"Yes, they even had a funeral for her, with her own grave stone."

May and William smiled and looked into each other's eyes, as Grace sensed an entire conversation passed between them with that one short gaze. "See, William," May looked up with an I-told-you-so twinkle in her eyes, "and you said it was silly to name our little boy."

"William Christopher Clark Jr. would have been his name, if he had been a boy," Dr. Clark reflected sorrowfully, but with a choking pride that seemed to stick in his throat.

"And of course he would have followed in his father's footsteps and become a doctor, just like my William," May added proudly.

A reflective silence engulfed the room at that moment, as Grace's thoughts drifted to the 'what ifs', of how much fuller and richer all of their lives would have been if Jeni and William Jr. had been allowed to live.

"Good morning, Grace," May said, as Grace entered the kitchen, drawn by the aroma of coffee and flapjacks on the grill. "William told me how much you Americans like your coffee, so I've put the tea away for the time being."

"Oh, you didn't have to do that," Grace said with appreciation as she sat down under the arches of an elegant but quaint breakfast area with large windows that reached from floor to ceiling. She gazed as though in a dream at the amazing view of the crashing waves of the North Atlantic and the majestic lighthouse situated at the end of the breakwater, the very one she had admired on the way there.

"William will be down shortly," May said, as she noticed Grace looking around the room hesitantly, wondering if she should start breakfast without Dr. Clark there to join them. "You go ahead and eat before your jacks get cold," May insisted, noticing Grace's forlorn, uneasy look. "Once William started again on those files you sent, he couldn't put them down. I could hardly get to sleep myself with all the excitement of his 'uh-hums', 'yes's' and 'maybes' he muttered all night."

"Then he thinks there's hope?"

"Grace, if I didn't already know my William's middle name was Christopher, I'm sure it would be Sanguine. He's known as 'The Miracle Worker' to all his colleagues, so your Piper is in the best hands she could be, except for maybe God Almighty's Himself. How's your little angel doing?"

"Well, Frank said she's doing fine, but I'm not sure. I get a sense that, that . . ."

"Well, if your husband said she's doing fine, she's doing fine. You just relax, finish your breakfast, and be ready to get to work when William comes down."

"Did I hear my name?" Dr. Clark called out as he entered the kitchen, "Mmmm, everything smells so good, Sweet May!"

"Yes dear, we were just talking about you, or at least I was talking to Grace about you."

"Sounds like so far you two have had rather a dull morning then," Dr. Clark quipped with a chuckle. "Good morning, Grace, I hope you slept well."

"I did; thank you so much. But I heard you didn't sleep so well yourself."

"Has May been tattling on me?" Dr. Clark answered, with a playfully glance at his wife.

Grace again admired the Clarks' charming and enduring interaction.

"Are you ready to get to work?" Dr. Clark added a little impatiently. "I already have several ideas I would like to go over with you; I found your 'Dream notes' fascinating!"

"If you are," Grace said, gathering her dishes.

"Now you just leave those to me, dear," May insisted, as she rushed over to take the items from Grace. "You and William have enough work to do, so you just go on."

May shooed Grace out of the kitchen as if she were some kind of meddlesome cat, for which Grace was grateful; her mind was anxious to hear Dr. Clark's preliminary thoughts, as well as that haunting, persistent, doubt that things at home weren't as they seemed. She sensed a hint of impatient eagerness; an uneasy urgency in Frank's voice, that belied his assurances and gave the impression that all was not as well, in spite of his assertions to the contrary.

Given time, Grace might have thought through the oxymoronic paradox of Frank's inconsistency; however, between her intense focus on finding that elusive cure, and Dr. Clark's barrage of questions relating to her and Frank's previous research, her feelings of uneasiness faded quickly into the background.

CHAPTER 19

Not a Wasted Dream

"I SEE YOU'VE WORKED with some very prominent colleagues of mine," the doctor began. And then, more rhetorically, "I assume, however, with no significant findings."

"Yes, we were fortunate to have such great help from very talented doctors, but after a while, getting nowhere, they just gave up."

"Well, don't give up hope," Dr. Clark said with confidence, "Today, or tomorrow, this week or next, we will change all that."

But, how could Grace not be discouraged? She and Frank had been at this for years with no workable solution. Still, she couldn't deny a resurgent feeling of optimism and confidence in Dr. Clark; so, riding on the coattails of this newfound hope, Grace dove confidently into this new effort with increased energy and confidence.

If she had known how things were at home, however, who knows how quickly her new optimism would have lasted.

"Life-support! An induced coma? Are you sure, Dr. Peterson? Piper's condition has deteriorated to that extent?" Frank asked with a fearful astonishment.

"Frank, I think it's time to give Grace a call," Alan suggested, upon hearing this latest news.

"Not yet," Frank answered, unwilling to keep Grace from even one moment of her work with Dr. Clark.

"If Grace and Dr. Clark are unable to find the answer soon, it's hopeless," Dr. Peterson said soberly, summing up the consultation.

Oh God, Give Dr. Clark and my Gracie your eternal wisdom . . . Frank prayed, sitting alone with Piper later that night. *And you, Piper,* he continued as he picked up her frail hand in his, *I command you, in Jesus's name, to hold on until help arrives . . .*

"Grace, as I continue to review your research, I find myself being continually drawn back to the Dream Notes you compiled with my Dream Son," Dr. Clark said, looking up from the plethora of papers he had printed out from Grace and Frank's years of work.

"But I think we've done all we can here. It's time to go see this daughter of yours in person."

"You would do that? Go all that way to see Piper?" Dumbfounded, Grace responded.

"Yes, of course," Dr. Clark sounded somewhat amused. "You didn't think I could develop a cure for a child without an in-person examination, did you?"

"Well I, ah, I didn't know what to think." Grace stammered.

"Well, you know what to think now," Dr. Clark chuckled, looking at a bewildered Grace. "You make the arrangements with your hubby, and I'll let May know we will be on the next plane to the States."

"You will be here when?" Frank answered Grace, as she explained Dr. Clark's planned in-person visit.

Grace noticed immediately a hesitation in her husband's voice. "What is it, Frank?" She demanded. "Is Piper . . . is she?"

"No, no, Grace," Frank reassured Grace, realizing his hesitation, had caused Grace to assume the worst. "She's struggling, but still with us. However, we're not at home." Frank shrank from uttering his next words. "Bring Dr. Clark to Mercy."

"Mercy!" Grace shouted into the phone, getting May and William's attention. "Why? What's wrong?" Grace demanded. "Why didn't you call me right away? How could you do this to me?"

By this time Grace was standing and was greatly agitated. Seeing Grace's anxiety and distress, May put a consoling arm around her.

"I hate him!" she blurted out, "I hate him . . ."

"No, you don't," May said, countering Grace's emotional vent, and helping her, trembling and distressed, back to the couch. "I'm sure whatever your husband did was for the best. You'll see—everything will be alright."

Grace and Dr. Clark arrived just twelve hours later. Grace had had time to calm down, and understand Frank and Alan's benevolent reasoning behind keeping Piper's true condition a secret from her. She had to admit that under the circumstances, they were right in that had they told her of Piper's actual state of health, she would have been on the next plane home. Dr. Clark even confirmed that those extra days granted to them were invaluable and possibly life-saving days.

"What do you think, Dr. Clark," Dr. Peterson asked, an hour after he had stepped off the plane. They were in the hospital's conference room, which was filled with staff and family, following a thorough examination of Piper by Dr. Clark.

"Well," Dr. Clark began, with a tone of confidence that put everyone at ease, "I think what I have to say has far less to do with me, and more to do with Grace and my Dream Son."

At the mention of Dr. Clark having a Dream Son the room immediately became a buzz of inarticulate voices, murmurs and stares; that is, accept for Grace, Alan and her family. They sat in anticipation as to what the doctor was eluding to.

After the buzz of curiosity as to what he meant by his Dream Son had settled down, Dr. Clark continued. "Not all of you know that Grace, Piper's mother, had a dream a few months back, and in her dream, she sought out a doctor by the name of Dr. William C. Clark."

The room again erupted in amazed murmurs but quieted down quickly, so they could finish hearing the doctor's explanation.

"In her dream, Grace traveled to Africa and found this Dr. Clark. They worked out a cure for her daughter, and she saw her grow healthy and strong, only to reawaken to the nightmare she is experiencing now. But I have good news—not only for Grace and Piper—but for all who have clung to hope and a belief that Providence would ultimately prevail in this case." He then turned to Grace, his eyes filled with a mist of relief and gratitude. "Grace," he said, "It was not a wasted dream, and my son, my Dream Son, if I had allowed him to live, would have been the doctor here conveying this good news to you in person." Everyone could hear the sentiment in his voice rise, as his frame visibly shook with emotion. "But alas," he went on, "that is a discussion for another time. Grace," he said, raising his tear-filled eyes to hers, "God in His wonderful mercy, has, through your dream, allowed my son, who I know without a shadow of a doubt is with Jesus as I speak, to mercifully unveil the mystery of Piper's illness to you."

Sobbing, Grace covered her face with her hands and wept tears of joy. *Miracle, a miracle,* was her only thought . . .

CHAPTER 20

The Ultimate Cure

"MAMA, IS THAT YOU?" A timid voice called out with searching eyes, trying to focus in the dimly lit room. Grace had adjusted herself in her chair to get more comfortable, making a grinding noise on the floor, thus waking Piper.

"Piper! You're awake! Frank! Piper's awake!" Grace cried out, in spite of the eerie quiet of the night, and the silence of the hospital corridors.

Frank and Alan, who had been rotating vigilance over Piper ever since the coma-inducing drugs had been discontinued, raced into the room.

"What ha . . . happened, wh . . . where am I?" Piper asked, even more alert now due to her mother's excited cries.

"You are in a hospital," Grace answered, showering her daughter with hugs and kisses. "But you are going to get well now!"

Frank and Alan also joined in on the loving caresses, covering Piper with even more hugs and kisses.

Grace was still somewhat bothered by Frank and Alan's deception, but she was too exuberant over finally hearing Piper's voice and seeing the life in her eyes after all these weeks, to hold any grudge at that moment. This was especially true about Alan, whose tragic loss in her dream, was still felt keenly in her memory. She knew instinctively that the decision her husband and Alan had made was the right one, but the emotional sting of betrayal still lingered; that is, until a few days later.

"That was a wise move," Dr. Clark remarked during a conference to update everyone on Piper's progress. Turning to Dr. Peterson, and congratulating him on his quick-minded decision to induce Piper's coma, he added, "It bought us the time we needed."

"Yes, I saw no other way to slow her rapidly failing condition at the time."

Piper's condition, now called Piper Syndrome, was improving rapidly, thanks to the vaccine derived from Grace's dream doctor, Dr. William C. Clark Jr.

"And you too, Frank," Grace stammered, "for, for having the courage to . . ."

"Well, now that Piper is on the path to recovery," Dr. Clark interrupted during Grace's long pause to keep her from having a publicly awkward moment. "I think it is time to give the One who is ultimately the true healer thanks as well; after all, it was through Him that my son . . . my should-have-been son, well . . ."

This time it was Grace's turn to return the favor by thanking everyone, especially Frank, for all the hard work, time, and sacrifices that had brought this ultimate healing to fruition. The road had not been easy, but they had seen how God had woven this miracle healing, thread-by-thread, through a myriad of physical and spiritual means, to bring health and vitality to Piper. God had not caused Piper's illness, but showed, by different means, and through different people, His mercy and faithfulness.

Soon Piper was up and around, laughing, playing and skipping down the hallways. There were so many 'Deja vu' moments for Grace that mimicked her dream that at times it felt like she was still in it. But was she still in a dream? No, not this time; this time it was the real thing.

"Hi May, this is my mother, Gloria, the woman I told you about, the one who had a crazy dream just like me," Grace said, as they stepped in to the Clarks' home, followed by a lively, energetic Piper, wide-eyed and overwhelmed with all the sights and wonders of this new world to which she was being introduced.

"William dear, would you mind taking Piper outside to the garden along the beach and see if she can find some nice souvenirs while I talk with Grace and her mother for a while?" May asked after formal introductions had been concluded.

"I would love to have that honor," Dr. Clark said with a grand, majestic flourishing of his hand, in an animated gesture as though to a queen. "How does that sound, Piper?"

"Great, Uncle William!" Piper, with excited anticipation, answered as she grabbed the doctor's hand, practically pulling him off his feet, through the back door and toward the beach.

"And to think just a few months ago you didn't even know if she was going to live," May said in reflective amazement, as they watched the pair bang their way through the screen door and out to the garden.

"Yes, Praise God, I still can't believe it," Grace said, with a mist in her eyes. "It's too wonderful for words."

"I never had the privilege of having grandchildren," May said, turning to Gloria. "I'm sure this ordeal was hard on you as well."

"Thank you for that, May. It was hard, not just to see Piper suffering the way she did, but to see my own Grace, and how she suffered. The worst for me, though, was to witness the hopelessness and despair when they would hit a brick wall, and then have no clue as to the next step."

"But we always had the Lord to turn to in those moments, didn't we, Mom?"

"Yes, Gracie, we did."

"I am so excited!" Grace said, diverting the conversation to the reason they were there in the first place. "I haven't heard the story of my little sister since I was a kid myself."

"May, when Grace told me how much you were still suffering about your son William, even after all these years, I wanted to meet with you and see if my own search for peace, after aborting my little Jeni, might be of help to you as well," Gloria added.

"Thank you so much for taking the time to visit with me and come all this way, Gloria," May said, and then turned to Grace. "And thank you, Grace, for thinking of me and the empathy you had to notice my deep sorrow that I still carry over what I did to William Jr."

Grace and Gloria spent the afternoon with May, getting to know her, as Gloria related her dream with them; about the stranger known as the Captain, who turned out to be Jesus, Skeeta and Skoota, Alan and Elle, and how she woke up devastated to realize what she had done.

"I actually had two dreams, May. In the first one, God allowed me to live a life with my little Jeni, and showed me what might have been, but in the second, He let me see what is; and at this very moment my daughter is alive and well, in the loving arms of her Captain, Jesus."

"Does that mean . . . William Jr. is . . ."

That is exactly what I mean! Whether a child is aborted, or there's a miscarriage, or even if we don't understand the reason; each one is with Jesus. Even your William Jr."

"That sounds so wonderful. I would like to hear more about that second dream," May asked, "If it isn't getting too late that is?"

"Not at all, May; I'd love to share it, and we'll just let time take care of itself," Gloria agreed enthusiastically. "It always brings me closer to my Jeni when I have an opportunity to tell stories about her."

"I wish I could think that way. All I've done is try to forget and bury my thoughts of William Jr. all these years."

"That will change; I know it," Gloria confidently assured May. "If you give that pain and self-reproach to Jesus, and know that not only Jesus forgives you, but William Jr. has as well, you will start to . . ."

"William?" May reacted with a jolt, astounded by this never-thought-of-before notion, that her aborted child could actually forgive her!

"Yes!" Gloria went on to emphasize this new reality to May. "I know once you understand, like I did, you will lovingly embrace the memory of William Jr., instead of hiding your face and running from him."

"Gloria, I'm more than ready. Tell me your dream," she insisted.

May listened eagerly as Gloria began . . .

"Well, I was in a courtroom, and there was a white-bearded old Judge with intense eyes looking down at me as he sat behind a very tall bench. Suddenly, the courtroom became a flurry of activity, as the Judge hit the bench with his gavel and commanded, "Bring in the witnesses!"

"Someone opened a door, and maybe a thousand or so people, started to file into the courtroom. A smartly dressed man was talking to the judge and pointing first at me, and then at the people coming through the door. The more they talked, the more irritated the Judge became."

"Then, I started to recognize a few of the people as they came in. There was a teacher that had once caught me cheating on a test, an old boss I had stolen from and even my husband was there! Then, an eerie silence came over the room, as a girl walked in, a girl not much older than Piper is now. She looked curiously around the room with searching eyes, until she saw me. Instantly, at that moment she recognized me, she smiled this loving smile that you had to see to know the warmth and wonder in it!"

"Mom?" She screamed, as she ran to me. "Is it you?"

"It was my Jeni . . ."

Taking a Kleenex from a box on the table, Gloria paused, as the retelling of her dream for the first time in so many years overwhelmed her with emotions she had held at bay for so long.

"I'm sorry," Gloria apologized, as May and Grace looked on, imagining what that moment must have been like for Gloria. Two hands of sympathy and comfort reached out to her as she continued.

"It was my grown-up little girl; and the shock of it caused me to faint and collapse on the floor.

"The first thing I heard when I woke up was, 'Mommy, I forgive you, I forgive you, Mommy!' Her loving arms went around me, and tears were falling from her eyes.

"Then, I heard another voice, 'I forgive you too, my daughter,' Someone said, as He lifted me to my feet. It was Jeni's Captain— Jesus; I recognized Him from my first dream. A peace I'd never experienced before came over me the moment He touched me. And as soon as He said I was forgiven, that slick-dressed man who had been arguing with the Judge looked so angry, I think he could have killed me right there on the spot. For a moment I was frightened, but soon everyone was gone, even that wretched man. The court-room was eerily quiet again."

"Where are your accusers?" Jesus asked with a radiant, inde-scribable smile.

"They . . . they've all gone, sir," I answered. Amazed, I didn't know what to think.

"Neither do I condemn you. Go in peace."

"I love you, Mama, but I have to go now," Jeni said, giving me one last hug, as she tenderly threw her arms around me and of-fered me one last goodbye kiss. "We will see each other again soon though, so very soon."

"I gave my darling baby one last, lingering hug, before she ran from my sight, and the big courtroom door closed behind her."

"To my surprise, I wasn't crying. The euphoria I felt at that moment was unbelievable, and even more unexplainable!" Gloria concluded.

I want that, May said to herself as she sat speechless, taking in the significance of what Gloria's dream could mean to her and her husband's peace of mind. *Jesus can cure so much more than a sick body.* May continued to ponder Gloria's story in the solitude of her mind. *He can also heal a sick heart.*

"You will never guess what," Frank said, as Grace and Piper walked in the door after returning from Canada and a quick stop at the doctor's office. "Alan called this afternoon and kept going on and on about this new woman he met. It was Joe this and Joe that . . ."

"Joe?" Grace interrupted, astonished and a little confused.

"From what he said, she has blonde hair too," Frank added with a laugh to drive home the peculiarity of the coincidence even further.

"Is that the same Joe from your dream, Mama?" Piper inquired innocently.

"No, Piper, dear," Grace answered with an amusing smile, "But maybe Dr. William C. Clark Jr. wasn't the only person in my dream who was destined to change our lives forever. I have my own surprise . . ."

"Mama's gonna have a baby, like in her dream!" Piper interrupted.

"Actually two," Grace corrected.

"Twins?" Frank exclaimed. "What next?"

LET ME LIVE

If I took another's breath away,
If I took their food, so they would waste away,
And if I made their heart cease to beat,
Or with a knife, made their flesh to bleed,
What would a jury's verdict be?
What would that victim say to me?

Let me live, let me live, let me live to see another day,
Let me live to see my mother's face I pray, let me live.

A million martyrs this year may fall,
Each death justified by freedom's call.
And each drop of blood cries to the throne of God,
While the judgment of each one falls on us all.
Now what would that jury's verdict be?
Their innocence cries out to you and me

Let me live, let me live, let me live to see another day,
Let me live to see my mother's face I pray, let me live.

And their silent screams, though not heard by man,
Are heard by the heavenly angel band as they sing

Oh come, angel band, Come and around me stand,
Carry me away on your snow-white wings to my eternal home,
Carry me away on your snow-white wings to my eternal home.

COPYRIGHT 2011 - eternalsoulministries.com

LOOKING BACK

My mother told me the other day,
Just before the Lord took her away.
Son, I never told you before,
But, you were almost never born.

I was young and all alone,
And had to choose between right and wrong.
Give you up to hide my shame,
Or give you life and bear the pain.

Looking back, I see all the faces,
Of friends and places that I would have missed.
Looking back, though sometimes through pain,
I would not have known love like this,
Looking back, looking back, I have no regrets,
Looking back.

Looking down upon her face,
I see the peace of God's grace.
And I'm glad she chose to let me live,
'Cause of all the love that we shared through it.

Looking back, I see all the faces
Of friends and places that I would have missed.
Looking back, though sometimes through pain,
I would not have known love like this,
Looking back, looking back, I have no regrets,
Looking back.

A MOTHER'S LAMENT

Jeni as a young girl wasn't always an angel.
But, oh how much I loved her through it all.
And, no matter how hard the hard times,
we were always there for each other.
I'm so glad she came into my life.

Jeni stands today, Michael by her side,
Hand in hand to say their wedding vows.
But, something doesn't seem right,
I feel it deep inside,
As I awake to see a doctor's face, I realize.

Jeni won't marry Michael in this lifetime,
'Cause, Jeni won't be around to say, "I do."
Jeni won't marry Michael in this lifetime.
'Cause I made that choice for her,
But I thought that I was making it for me.

Now, I was told just another choice,
To be made in the name of freedom.
So, why do I feel so lonely in my soul?
Could it be I was mistaken, as I walk out of this door?
'Cause I'll never see my Jeni anymore.

Jeni won't marry Michael in this lifetime,
'Cause, Jeni won't be around to say, "I do."
Jeni won't marry Michael in this lifetime.
'Cause I made that choice for her,
But I thought that I was making it for me.

"Praise God from whom all blessings flow."

LEE GANDER WAS CALLED to the ministry at an early age, and has dedicated his life to preaching the Good News, setting the captive free, and championing the innocent, those silent voices that cannot speak for themselves. A prolific writer of over 400 songs and an accomplished musician, Lee is now venturing in this new direction as author, with a desire to passionately broaden the message of God's redemptive love for the lost and hurting around him.

www.ingramcontent.com/pod-product-compliance
Lightning Source LLC
Chambersburg PA
CBHW060810250626
47162CB00005B/1734